Dead in the Dinghy

Dead in the Dinghy

A MOLLIE MCGHIE SAILING MYSTERY #4

ELLEN JACOBSON

For all the cats out there who love nothing
more than waking up their humans at the crack of
dawn to demand their breakfast. There's nothing quite
like a furry alarm clock pawing at your face to
get you going in the morning.

CONTENTS

THE CREW

MOLLIE MCGHIE – When she isn't investigating murders and learning how to sail, Mollie spends her time educating the public about UFOs and alien abduction.

SCOOTER MCGHIE – Mollie's husband. Passionate about boats, he dreams about sailing around the world one day.

MRS. MOTO – Mollie and Scooter's Japanese bobtail cat who has an uncanny talent for finding clues.

JIM FERGUSON – Owner of the Sailor's Corner Cafe.

PENNY CHADWICK – runs the local sailing school and boat brokerage.

OLIVIA PETERSON – World-famous sailor, YouTube celebrity, and artist.

ALAN SIMPSON – Wedding photographer, YouTuber, and aspiring photojournalist.

NED & NANCY SCHNEIDER – Owners of the Palm Tree Marina.

THOMAS SINCLAIR – Runs a retreat for artists on Destiny Key.

GREGOR SMIRNOV – Owner of art galleries around the world, including one in Coconut Cove.

BEN MORETTI – A wannabe pirate who works at the marina.

CHIEF "TINY" DALTON – Coconut Cove's chief of police.

ANABEL DALTON – Chief Dalton's ex-wife; local artist known for her fanciful paintings.

FRICK & FRACK – The Dalton's adorable Yorkshire terrier dogs.

VICTORIA WILLIAMS – Local artist known for her seascapes.

MELVIN ROLLE – Owner of Melvin's Marine Emporium; originally from the Bahamas.

SAWYER NICHOLS – Local singer and artist who lives in a converted van.

CHIEF ARCHIBALD TYLER – Destiny Key's chief of police.

TANNER – Barista at the cafe on Destiny Key.

SILAS DE VRIES – Art collector who lives on Destiny Key.

CHAPTER 1
HONEY-DO LISTS

What would you do if your husband decided to start a YouTube channel featuring your cat? Would you:

(a) Give him a honey-do list because clearly he has too much time on his hands;

(b) Search for a product to tame your frizzy hair in case you end up on camera;

(c) Worry that your cat was going to develop an over-sized ego; or

(d) Start sewing adorable cat costumes?

Option (a) was very tempting. I love creating to-do lists. Doing the tasks on them, not so much. That's what makes honey-do lists so appealing—you get to assign chores to your hubby while you sit back, relax, and eat chocolate.

If only that was how it worked. Sigh. In reality, both Scooter and I had huge to-do lists already. Neither of us had time to chill out and eat chocolate. Okay, the part about not eating chocolate? A total lie. I always find time for chocolate. Having lots that needs to be done? That's true. You see, we live on a dilapidated sailboat named *Marjorie Jane*. We've been spending lots of time and money fixing her up, but it seems like a never-ending battle. How that man is going to manage to find time between the boat and his telecommunications business to turn our cat into an internet sensation is beyond me.

There are days when *Marjorie Jane* makes me want to tear my hair out, which brings me to option (b)—my quest for a miracle product that will make my tresses smooth and silky so that I would be camera-ready. I can't tell you how many jars, tubes, and bottles I've bought from hairdressers over the years. Nothing has worked so far. I probably should resign myself to my mousy-brown frizz. It does a halfway decent job of camouflaging my oddly shaped skull, the result of one too many crashes back in my roller derby days.

Our cat, Mrs. Moto, doesn't have to worry about how she looks. She's a gorgeous Japanese bobtail calico with glossy fur and black markings around her eyes that resemble glasses. While she loves being the center of attention, I wasn't too worried about (c)—having to deal with a feline diva. So far, her ego seems to be in check, at least by cat standards. After all, don't all cats already believe they're the center of the universe since being told they were gods by the ancient Egyptians?

Option (d) was definitely going to happen. Mrs. Moto loved to dress up almost as much as I loved to dress her up. In fact, she had recently won the annual Coconut Cove pet costume competition. Her Princess Leia outfit had wowed the judges. I couldn't wait to get my sewing machine out and make a little sailor suit for her. Scooter was enthusiastic about the idea. He thought it would be a great look for her debut video.

Which brings me back to this whole hare-brained scheme of his to make Mrs. Moto a YouTube star. Why don't you grab a beverage and some cookies, and I'll tell you all about how he sprung this little surprise on me.

There we were, sipping our morning coffee in *Marjorie Jane's* cockpit and watching the sun rise over the dusty boatyard. My stomach grumbled loudly. It does that on a regular basis, reminding me that it needs regular feedings. I wasn't looking forward to breakfast—a piece of whole wheat toast with a poached egg. Yuck. Over the past few months, we had been trying to eat healthier, but there are only so many days in a row you can survive without sugar and bacon. Not necessarily together, but you know what I mean. So when Scooter suggested we go to the Sailor's Corner Cafe, I was overjoyed. Thoughts of pancakes drenched in butter and syrup made me salivate.

When we arrived at the cafe, I started to walk toward my favorite booth by the window. Scooter grabbed my elbow. "No, not there. We're going to the meeting room instead."

"Why's that?"

He steered me through the restaurant to a courtyard at the rear of the building. "You'll see," he said with a mysterious smile.

I clapped my hands together. "Ooh. A surprise! I love surprises."

"That's not what you said when I gave you *Marjorie Jane* for our tenth wedding anniversary."

"Well, rundown sailboats don't usually top my list of things I want to be surprised with," I said. "But I'm sure this one will be great."

He smiled. "I think you're going to love it."

The scent of gardenias filled the air as we walked across the brick patio toward the meeting room. As Scooter put his hand on the door handle, I asked, "Should I close my eyes?"

He furrowed his brow. "Why? That would make it hard to see."

"But it's customary," I said, squeezing my eyes shut. "Then everyone yells, 'Surprise!' and you open your eyes in astonishment."

"Uh, I don't think that's a good idea. There are a couple of steps down into the room. You could trip."

I opened my eyes and shrugged. "Okay, we'll play it your way. At least let me guess what's inside. Obviously, there's a chocolate cake and—"

"It's eight o'clock," he interrupted. "Why would there be cake so early?"

"You're the one who scheduled my little surprise for the morning. But that's fine with me. Cake tastes just as good for breakfast as it does in the evening. Let's see, what else will there be..." I tapped my finger against my lips. "Clowns," I said decisively. "There are clowns inside too."

"Clowns?" Scooter spluttered. "Why would there be clowns?"

"Oh, you're good. Pretending like you don't know what I'm talking about." I squeezed his arm. "I almost believed you."

"Honestly, I'm not pretending." He pulled open the door. "We're going to be late. Let's head inside."

As I entered the large room, I noted a distinct lack of decorative touches. A large screen was positioned at the front next to a podium and a small table with a laptop and a pitcher of water. Dotted around the room were round tables covered in plain white tablecloths, with notepads and pens at each place setting. No flowers, no streamers, no balloons, and not a single clown in sight.

Scooter pointed at a buffet at the side of the room. "Why don't we grab a bite to eat before it starts?"

"Count me in," I said. "Chocolate cake and coffee. The perfect way to start the day." As I threaded my way through a group of young men talking about microphones and tripods, I wondered why there were people I didn't know in attendance. Before I could ask about the invite list, Jim Ferguson, the owner of the Sailor's Corner Cafe, pulled Scooter aside. Jim's usual appearance always made me think of what Santa Claus would look like if he were on vacation in Florida. A bushy white beard, a portly physique, bright red cheeks, a Hawaiian shirt, shorts, and sandals.

While Scooter and Jim were deep in conversation—no doubt making sure all the arrangements for my surprise were in place—I surveyed the breakfast options. Miniature seemed to be the theme of the day. I piled mini quiches, mini pigs-in-a-blanket, mini waffles, and mini muffins onto my plate. Fortunately, the bacon strips were full-sized.

As I reached across the table for a mini doughnut, a familiar voice said, "Maybe you should save room for dessert." I looked up and saw my friend, Penny Chadwick, holding a fruit kebab. As usual, she was dressed head-to-toe in her favorite color, pink. Even her long blond hair was pulled back with a pink bow.

"Only you would think fruit was a suitable dessert," I said with a smile. "I'll be having the chocolate cake instead."

"It's a little early for cake, don't you think?" she asked with that adorable Texan twang of hers.

"You're right. It is too early." I pointed at Scooter, who was still talking with Jim. "He's probably arranging for it to be brought out after everyone has had their breakfast."

"He is?"

I leaned toward her and said in a low voice, "It's okay. I know about the surprise party."

"Surprise party?" Penny cocked her head to one side. "Wait a minute, is it your birthday today?"

"No, not until next month."

"Then why would Scooter throw you a surprise party today?"

"Duh. That's what would make it so surprising," I said. "I have to say, he's been really clever about it. If you look around the room, you wouldn't think it's a party."

"That's because it isn't—"

A voice over the speakers interrupted Penny. "Could everyone please take their seats?" A young woman with neon blue cropped hair and ruddy skin was standing at the podium. "We're going to start the presentation in a few minutes."

"Who's that?" I asked, balancing my plate while I poured a cup of coffee.

"She's the guest speaker," Penny replied. "She flew down from New York City yesterday."

"Guest speaker? That's kind of an odd touch for a party."

"I think you might have your wires crossed." After Penny selected an herbal tea, she said, "It looks like Scooter snagged a table up front. Come on, let's sit down. I don't want to miss anything."

After taking our seats, the lights dimmed. Pictures of sailboats flashed across the screen, accompanied by upbeat music, before fading to a shot of the speaker at the helm of the boat and the words, "Olivia Peterson. Sailor. Artist. YouTuber." Everyone broke into applause as the lights came back on. Everyone except me. I was too busy deciding which miniature breakfast item to eat first.

"Welcome, everyone," the blue-haired woman said. "When Alan Simpson asked me to give a presentation, he thought five, maybe ten people would register." She pointed at a short man standing in the corner holding a camera. He wasn't hard to miss with his obviously-from-a-bottle chestnut hair. "Alan, it looks like you were wrong. Look at this crowd. What a great turnout." She pointed at the audience. "Give yourselves a hand, everyone!"

While everyone clapped, I looked around the room. Why didn't I know half of the people Scooter had invited to my party? And why had he asked Alan to organize a guest speaker? Before I could find out what was going on, she continued. "I'm sure you all already know a bit about me and my background, but just in case you don't, let me give you a little intro. My name is Olivia Peterson. I recently finished circumnavigating the globe on my sailboat, the *Anastasia*."

As the room broke out into applause again, Scooter leaned

over and whispered, "Isn't she amazing? That could be us one day."

"Circumnavigating? Yeah, right," I said as I dusted crumbs off my shirt. "Let's just concentrate on successfully sailing in the Coconut Cove Regatta this weekend before we make grand plans to take our boat any further afield."

"Shush," Penny said. "I can't hear her."

The young woman smiled and held up her hands. "Thank you, but you should be applauding yourselves, not me. You're the ones taking the first step toward being a creative entrepreneur by setting up your own YouTube channel." She motioned at Alan. He approached the podium, held his camera up, and panned the room from left to right. "By the way, Alan is going to be taking some B-roll footage during today's session, which I'll be using in my next video."

I frowned. I was okay with pictures of my party, but videos made me uncomfortable, especially since my hair was having an extra unruly day. There's nothing worse than seeing frizzy hair in motion.

Olivia grabbed a portable microphone, then walked over to our table. "Before we dive into my presentation, why don't we go around the room and do some introductions? Please tell us your name and what kind of videos you want to create."

I blinked rapidly. This was starting to seem less and less like a surprise party. Unless it was meant to be a really bad surprise party. When Olivia held the microphone in front of my husband, my fears were confirmed.

He stood and adjusted his tortoiseshell glasses. "Hi. My name is Scooter McGhie. My wife, Mollie, and I are starting a YouTube channel featuring our cat, Mrs. Moto."

I cleared my throat before asking, "We are?"

"It's exciting, isn't it?" Scooter said, his dark brown puppy dog eyes sparkling with excitement. He picked up a large envelope from the table, opened it up, pulled out a stack of glossy photographs, then handed one to Olivia.

"Oh my gosh," she said, holding it up for the audience to see. "She's so adorable."

I grabbed one of the photos. "Are these head shots of Mrs. Moto?"

"They turned out nicely, didn't they?" Scooter said with a huge grin plastered on his face.

I leaned back in my chair and sighed. My husband certainly had surprised me, just not in the way I had hoped.

While I contemplated Scooter's new fascination with cat videos, Olivia continued with introductions.

As Penny explained how she wanted to leverage YouTube to drive business to her sailing school and boat brokerage, I grabbed the last piece of bacon from Scooter's plate. He was so absorbed in looking at the pictures of our cat that he didn't even notice.

"That's a wonderful idea," Olivia said to Penny. "I have a number of friends who use their channels to generate new business leads. The trick is to post interesting content, not just advertisements for your business."

"I thought I'd start with filming the Coconut Cove Regatta," Penny said. "People might enjoy watching footage of the sailing races, as well as the other regatta events we have planned to celebrate the Fourth of July."

Olivia nodded. "Great idea. The regatta sounds like a lot of fun."

"There's always room for a famous circumnavigator on my boat," Penny said. "We'd love to have you on board."

"I wish I could join you, but I already have plans for the holiday weekend. I'll be at an artists' retreat on Destiny Key."

"That's where the regatta sails to," Penny said. "Maybe we'll see you there."

"I'll keep an eye out for your boat," the young woman replied. "What's her name?"

"*Pretty in Pink*," Penny said. "You can't miss it. She's all pink."

I listened half-heartedly during the rest of the introductions, perking up only when someone I knew was speaking. Alejandra Lopez, a waitress at the Sailor's Corner Cafe, explained how she wanted to do online tutorials on nail art. Ned Schneider, who owned the Palm Tree Marina with his wife Nancy, described his vision for a YouTube channel dedicated to movie reviews. In my opinion, Penelope Pringle had the best idea—behind-the-scenes videos of how she makes the delicious treats for sale at her bakery, the Sugar Shack.

Eventually, Olivia got to her presentation—two excruciating hours filled with more detail than I ever wanted to know about filming and editing videos, establishing your brand, and monetizing your content. Scooter took detailed notes, I played games on my phone, and, to my great disappointment, neither a chocolate cake nor clowns made an appearance.

* * *

"When were you going to tell me about this whole YouTube thing?" I asked Scooter after Olivia's presentation was over.

He scratched his head. "I did tell you. The other night when we were at the Tipsy Pirate."

"When was that?"

"Friday."

"Was I even there?"

"Of course you were. Remember, we went to the movies then stopped by for a bite to eat."

I stared at him blankly.

"You had the egg rolls with the pineapple dipping sauce."

"Oh, yeah. Now I remember. Those were delicious," I said. "Didn't Alan come over and join us?"

"Yes, and that's when we talked about the YouTube channel."

"We did?"

"Sure, Alan told us how he set up his own channel. You know, the one featuring his pet mice. Then he suggested Mrs. Moto would be a natural in front of the camera."

"Did I contribute to the conversation?"

"If you consider saying 'uh-huh' and 'um' a lot, then you contributed. Guess you were daydreaming again."

I shrugged. "Maybe."

"Let me guess. It was about aliens landing on—"

Before Scooter could finish his thought, Jim interrupted him. "Either one of you want this?" he asked, holding out a tray with a solitary mini muffin on it. "It's the last one left."

"Is that blueberry?" I asked.

Scooter smiled. "You're going to try to claim that because it has fruit in it. It's part of your five a day, isn't it?"

"It's called out-of-the-box thinking." I snatched the treat and took a nibble. "Yum. I can feel the antioxidants coursing through my body already."

"It's back to poached eggs and whole wheat toast for us tomorrow, my little stegosaurus."

"Stegosaurus?" Jim asked as he set the empty tray down on a nearby table.

"Yeah, it's his latest pet name for me," I said in between bites. "He's been watching too many documentaries about dinosaurs lately."

"That's, um, different," Jim said wryly.

"Trust me, it's an improvement on some of the other ones he's called me," I said.

"Speaking of pet names, there's my 'sweetie' now." Jim pointed at a dapper-looking man and waved him over. "Have you met Thomas before?"

While Scooter introduced himself, I admired the man's eclectic attire—a green plaid three-piece suit, a crisp white shirt, a brightly colored polka-dot bow tie, and a jaunty red beret perched on top of his salt and pepper hair. Not many people in Coconut Cove dressed so formally, preferring a more casual beach look.

As I shook Thomas' hand, I wondered how he coped in the intense Florida heat while wearing a suit. Then I looked at his feet and saw that he was wearing flip-flops. I guess if your feet can breathe, it helps cool the rest of you down.

"Thomas is an artist," Jim said proudly. "He paints these fantastic seascapes. You might have seen some of them on display in the cafe."

"Ah," I said. "That explains your cufflinks."

Thomas held up his wrists. "Aren't they cute? Little easels. Jim gave them to me last Christmas."

"I've noticed your paintings before. They're really striking," Scooter said. "It's too bad we live on a sailboat. We don't have any wall space to hang anything."

"I miss our cottage," I said with a sigh. "We used to have some really nice artwork. Not to mention a bathtub and a freezer. Do you know what life is like without ice cream at your fingertips?"

"But living on a boat must be so romantic," Thomas said.

Scooter put his arm around my shoulders. "It's been tough lately. *Marjorie Jane* has been in the boatyard for the last few months while we've been working on her, and living there has been—"

"The opposite of romantic," I said, finishing his sentence. "Climbing up and down a ladder multiple times a day, dust and dirt everywhere, tools and parts strewn all about ... it gets old after a while."

"But we're splashing our boat this afternoon," Scooter said. "Once she's back in the water things will get better. And we're sailing in the regatta this weekend. What could be more romantic than that?"

"I'd love to see your boat some time," Thomas said. "In addition to seascapes, I enjoy painting all kinds of boats—fishing boats, tugboats, sailboats, even rowboats. In fact, I'm running the artists' retreat on Destiny Key this weekend."

"The same one Olivia is going to?" Scooter asked.

He nodded. "If the weather cooperates, I'm planning on taking the group out to the beach to sketch the regatta boats at anchor. I'll have to keep an eye out for yours."

"She isn't hard to miss," I said. "Just look for the red-hulled boat with teak decks in serious need of varnish."

"I thought they weren't fond of outsiders on the island," Scooter said. "How did you manage to schedule your retreat there?"

"It's true. The locals are wary of outsiders," Thomas said. "But I have a friend who's traveling in Europe for the summer and he offered his house to me. It's in an absolutely exquisite location. The views are to die for. You feel like you're on some tropical island in the Pacific, rather than on an island off the Florida coast. It's an artist's dream. I couldn't pass it up." He leaned in and said in a confidential tone, "My friend is a bit of a Destiny Key rebel. I think he secretly likes the idea of inviting mainlanders to the island because he knows that it makes everyone furious. He especially likes sticking it to his cousin. They had a bit of a falling out a few years ago."

"But won't the locals give you a hard time while you're there?" I asked.

"Nah, it won't be too bad. We only have to deal with folks on the ferry. Once we get to the island, we'll head straight to the house. It's located out at the far end of the island in an isolated bay. No one around for miles. It's well stocked so we won't need to go into town for anything. The locals will barely know we're there. You should hear some of the names they have for us. They aren't very flattering."

"Having met someone from there and learned about the island, it actually doesn't surprise me," I said.

"Please. Let's not talk about what happened to her," Scooter said.

Thomas looked at Jim. "Is she talking about that horrible

incident that happened when I was in New York for the art show?"

"Yes, Mollie found the body." Jim turned to me. "How many bodies is that you've found now? Ten? Twelve?"

I scowled. "Why does everyone in Coconut Cove insist on keeping a tally of how many dead bodies I happen to run across?"

Jim chuckled. "Well, you do have a bit of a reputation."

"For the record, it's five." I glanced at Scooter, then breathed a sigh of relief. He didn't look like he was going to faint. My husband had a hard time dealing with anything gruesome. Even a little bit of blood from a paper cut could send him over the edge. So you can only imagine how he felt when there was a dead body involved. Usually a bit of chocolate helped restore his equilibrium, which is why I always kept an emergency supply of M&M'S in my purse.

"And your record is going to stay at five, right?" Scooter asked.

"Why stop at five?" Jim asked with a smile. "You should try to get into the *Guinness Book of World Records*."

"Oh, I already did that," I said.

Jim was taken aback. "You did?"

"Oh, no. Not for dead bodies or anything like that," I said. "It was for—"

Before I could finish explaining my world record, the door to the conference room swung open. A man stood regally in the entryway, surveying the room as though he was expecting his subjects to kneel in adoration. Like Thomas, he was also wearing a suit, but whereas Thomas' outfit was a riot of color, his was all black, including shirt and tie. Even his hair and eyes were black. The only spot of color was a mother-of-pearl handle on the cane he was leaning on.

"What's Gregor doing here?" Thomas hissed, his face turning the same bright-red color as his beret.

"I'm sure there's a perfectly reasonable explanation," Jim

said. "Don't let him upset you. Remember what your doctor said about your blood pressure."

Thomas clenched his fists. "I know what he said. But as long as Gregor is anywhere near me, there's no way I'm going to be able to avoid becoming stressed."

"Why don't you practice your breathing exercises?" Jim rested his hand on his stomach and slowly inhaled and exhaled. "Like this. In. Out. In. Out."

Thomas placed his hand on his own stomach, closed his eyes, and breathed deeply. As his color started to return to normal, Jim squeezed his shoulder. "You're doing great. Keep going."

While Thomas focused on his breathing, I noticed the man in black walking across the room, the tapping sound of his cane on the tile floor getting progressively louder as he neared us. "I think he's coming this way," I whispered to Scooter.

"Do you know who he is?" Scooter asked.

"Never seen him before. But he doesn't exactly look like the type to hang out at the marina."

"Well, I think we're going to have a chance to find out who he is," Scooter said. "He's making a beeline straight toward us."

As the man stopped in front of us, Thomas' eyes snapped open, his face flushing again.

"You should be more careful in the sun," Gregor said with a heavy accent that sounded Russian. "You are very sunburned."

Thomas narrowed his eyes. "What do you want?"

Gregor reached into the pocket of his suit jacket and pulled out an envelope. "I thought I would hand deliver this. You know how unreliable the mail service can be."

Thomas folded his arms across his chest. "I don't want anything from you."

"Very well," Gregor said. "I thought I would do you the

courtesy of delivering this to you personally, but, if you prefer, I will send it directly to your lawyer instead."

"Courtesy," Thomas said bitterly. "What would you know about courtesy? Do you think coming into *my* town and trying to destroy *my* reputation is courteous?"

Gregor gave him a slight smile. "I only speak the truth. You Americans are delicate creatures, no? You cannot bear it when someone gives you an honest critique of your talent. Or in your case, your lack of talent." He waved the envelope. "You are sure you are not the slightest bit curious about what is inside?"

"Give me that," Jim said, grabbing it out of his hand. He ripped open the envelope, pulling a thick document out. He silently leafed through the pages while Thomas glared at Gregor. After a few minutes, Jim took a deep breath and said to Thomas, "I think we are going to need a lawyer."

"Why? What does it say?" Thomas asked.

"He's claiming that you can't use Coconut Creations anymore for your art-related business. He's trademarked it."

Thomas looked like he was going to have a stroke. "What? Coconut Creations is mine. I've used it for years on my business cards, my website, and the art gallery. He can't take it away from me. It's my brand."

Gregor shrugged. "When you sold the art gallery to me, you gave up all rights to using the name."

"I didn't sell it to you, you stole it!"

"I am a businessman, not a thief. I cannot help it if you are unhappy with the transaction. Some people do not have a head for business." He tapped his cane on the floor sharply. "You have one week to comply."

Thomas ripped the document in half and dropped it on the floor. "That's what I think of your threats."

"You make mistake. Serious mistake," Gregor said. "My lawyers will take you to court. You will have nothing left after they finish. Nothing."

As he made his way toward the exit, Thomas said in a low undertone. "You'll pay for this. Just wait and see. You'll pay."

CHAPTER 2
CLAUSE 72(C)

After Gregor's dramatic departure, Jim hurried everyone out of the meeting room while Thomas paced back and forth, fuming over the letter from the lawyers.

Scooter and I returned to our boat to pick up Mrs. Moto. Having napped all morning, she was eager to go outside and play. The three of us walked to the patio area by the marina office. Or rather two of us walked, while the one of us with four legs raced down the path, stopping periodically to yowl at us to hurry up.

When we reached the boardwalk that separated the patio from the beach, Mrs. Moto briefly chased a seagull, then leaped onto one of the tables. Scooter set down the tote bag he had been carrying. The calico knocked the bag on its side, stuck her head inside, then pulled out some gray material.

"What's that?" I asked.

Scooter grabbed it from the cat and held it up. "I ordered it online. Isn't it cute?"

"Is that what I think it is?"

"Yep. A shark costume." He picked up Mrs. Moto and rubbed his nose against hers. "Are you ready to get dressed up?"

She meowed with delight as Scooter wrestled her into the costume.

While Mrs. Moto chased lizards on the patio, the fin on her back flipping back and forth as she pounced, I went into the office to settle our bill.

After months living on "the hard" in the boatyard, we were more than ready to splash *Marjorie Jane* back into the water and move her into a slip. I was looking forward to not having to climb up and down a ladder multiple times a day, and being able to enjoy the cooling breezes coming in off the bay and the gentle rocking back and forth in the water while I drifted off to sleep.

Despite the fact that I had never wanted a sailboat, *Marjorie Jane* had started to grow on me. I think when you invest as much time, sweat, and money as we have into a project boat, one of two things happens. Some folks end up so frustrated, tired, and broke that they secretly hope their boat accidentally burns down, insurance pays out, and they get to go off on a less stressful adventure, like RVing. For others, after investing so much of themselves into their "baby," they're bound and determined to enjoy all the improvements they've made and equipment they've bought. I was in the latter camp, eager to try out our new headsail during the race to Destiny Key. We had also purchased a new dinghy, which I wanted to take out for a spin.

Before I pushed the door to the marina office open, I practiced the breathing exercise Thomas and Jim had been doing. I needed to prepare myself mentally in order to deal with Nancy, Ned's wife and the co-owner of the Palm Tree Marina. She was the only thing standing in our way of splashing and moving into our slip. Given her love of bureaucracy, I expected the required paperwork was going to take every ounce of patience I had.

"Close the door," Nancy barked as I entered. "You're going to let the flies in." I quickly took a step back as she smacked a fly swatter down on the counter. The force of the blow caused a pen holder to fall down, its contents scattering across the floor and under the nearby display racks of nautical charts and cruising guides.

"Well," Nancy said, peering over her reading glasses. "Aren't you going to pick those up?"

"I didn't drop them," I said.

"They didn't fall down by themselves, did they, dear?"

"But you, you ..." I was at a loss for words and pointed at the fly swatter instead.

"Good, I like to see initiative," the older woman said as she handed me the swatter. "There are a couple of flies in the corner. You can take care of them after you pick the pens up. You're going to need one to sign your paperwork."

Before I could protest that I hadn't been offering to reduce the insect population in the office, let alone deal with the pens, the phone rang. Nancy answered it with a surprisingly cheerful tone—one I had only heard her use with her grandchildren—instead of with her usual brisk, no-nonsense manner.

I listened as she politely explained the marina fees to the caller. "Hold on one moment, sir," she said. "Let me make a note of that." She held the phone away from her ear, turned to me, and reached out her hand. "Hand me a pen, will you, dear."

I sighed, bent down, and scooped them up. Usually it was easier to give in to Nancy. I set the pens on the counter. She grabbed one, then scribbled something down on a piece of paper. "Okay, I'll look into it. Why don't you call back in a few minutes and I'll see what I can do."

After she hung up, I asked, "What do I need to sign for our new slip?"

She walked toward the file cabinets at the rear of the office. "I'll be with you in a minute," she said over her shoulder. "I have to sort something else out first. Why don't you put those pens back in the holder while you're waiting?"

I complied with her request, however I did put some of the pens in upside down and removed the caps from others. Sometimes, a minor act of rebellion can brighten up your day.

While she looked through file folders, I perused the brochures on display by the door. Most of them were geared toward tourists—bed and breakfast establishments, fishing boat charters, local restaurants, and guided visits to an alligator farm. As I pulled out the one for Pete's Gator Park for a closer look, I wondered what exactly went on at an alligator farm. Did the gators wear overalls, straw hats, and tend to crops of carrots and rutabagas? After studying the brochure, I learned that there wasn't any cultivation going on. Just photo ops with baby gators, a tram ride to see the big gators at the swamp at the back of Pete's place, and a gift shop.

After replacing it back on the rack, a glossy brochure next to it caught my eye. Gregor's Coconut Creations Art Gallery was printed on the top in an ornate script, followed by the hotly contested trademark sign. Gregor certainly was putting a stake in the ground that he had the rights to the Coconut Creations name.

Underneath the gallery name was a picture of what looked like an old railway station. The brickwork had been painted black, which contrasted with colorful flowers spilling out of large silver containers positioned by the entryway. When I flipped the brochure over and looked at the map on the back, I realized that it was located on the outskirts of Coconut Cove, near where the main road branched off. One direction took you toward the "big city." The other took you to a dock where the ferry to Destiny Key departed from.

On the inside of the brochure were pictures of paintings and sculptures tastefully displayed in the gallery, along with a photo and bio of Gregor. He was Russian, as I had suspected. Originally from Saint Petersburg, he had emigrated to New York City where he founded an art school and opened his first art gallery. Over the years he had acquired galleries around the world, with Coconut Creations being the latest jewel in his crown.

While I thought about what it would be like to have artistic talent, Nancy grabbed a thick stack of papers from the printer. She set them down on the counter with a flourish. "This is the new contract for your slip rental. Initial in the sections indicated, then sign and date the last page."

"I might need some coffee to keep me awake while I read all of this," I said.

Her piercing blue eyes bored into me. "You don't need to read it. Just sign and initial."

"Scooter always says it's important to read legal documents thoroughly," I said, furrowing my brow.

Nancy shrugged. "Suit yourself. Don't take too long though. There's only one slip left and I need a signed contract before I can assign it to you. First come, first serve."

"What? Ned said it was ours. He reserved it for us."

The older woman pursed her lips. "He shouldn't have done that. I'm the one in charge of the office. He's in charge of the fuel dock and maintenance. Besides, if you look at clause 34(a), you'll see the section about slip assignments. No reservations."

I sighed as I flipped through the pages. It all seemed like pretty standard fare—no discharge of chemicals overboard, liability insurance requirements, loud parties strictly forbidden—that sort of thing. Then I reached section 72(c): "Residents of the marina are not allowed to use the patio grill to cook beef. Only chicken, fish, and tofu are permitted."

"What's this beef clause about?" I asked. "We always grill hamburgers at the weekly potluck."

She pulled the contract toward her and peered at the page.

"Oh, that. Ned needs to watch his cholesterol."

"But what does that have to do with the rest of us?" I asked.

"If he smells steak and burgers cooking, he'll be tempted to have some."

I smiled. In a weird, controlling way, clause 72(c) was Nancy's way of showing that she cared for her husband. "So, because you're worried that he doesn't have any willpower, the rest of us have to suffer," I said.

"They have these new vegetarian burgers nowadays. You can make those instead." She tapped the page with her pen. "You know what I forgot to include? No cheese allowed either." She started to scribble something down to that effect when the phone rang again.

"Yes, we have one slip left," she said to the person on the other end of the line. "How big is your boat? Yes, that shouldn't be a problem. Just email the signed contract back and it's all yours. You sent it already? Just a moment, let me check." As she walked toward the computer, I quickly signed and initialed my contract and shoved it in her hands.

"I believe that slip is ours," I said. Before she could protest, I added, "Like you said, 'first come first serve.' I was here first."

She sniffed, then nodded. After explaining to the caller that they'd have to find another marina, she put my signed contract in a file folder. "I'm surprised you didn't have any questions about section 83(d)."

"83(d)?" I spluttered. "What was that one about?"

Nancy placed the folder into a file cabinet. "No hanging clothes out on your boat."

I rolled my eyes. That one I could live with, but I wasn't sure how my friend, Ben Moretti, would react. His boat was definitely not in compliance when it came to laundry. Rather than spend his money on the dryer, he often strewed his clothes on deck to dry in the sun.

"You're all set," Nancy said, tapping her perfectly manicured fingernails on the counter.

"Good. We've got a lot to get done before the regatta starts on Friday."

"Do you really think you and Scooter are up for a regatta? You've had that boat less than a year and it's been in the boatyard for most of that time." She shook her head. "And neither of you have any real sailing experience."

"Hey, I've been taking sailing lessons with Penny," I protested.

"It's not the same thing as sailing your own boat, let alone racing in it."

I felt my stomach knotting up. When I signed us up for the regatta, it had seemed like a good idea. But, now, as the time neared, I was starting to worry if we were really up for it. However, there was no way I was going to let Nancy know that I was concerned.

"It will be fine," I said resolutely. "Besides, Ben and Melvin are going with us."

"Humph. Ben isn't exactly the type of person I'd entrust my safety to. He's like Peter Pan. Never grew up."

She did have a point. Ben lived paycheck-to-paycheck, his sailboat was so rundown that it actually made *Marjorie Jane* look good in comparison, and his wardrobe consisted of tattered shorts and t-shirts with pirate slogans on them. But, on the plus side, he knew his way around boats and could fix just about anything. When I said as much to Nancy, she reluctantly agreed.

"The customers are satisfied with the work he does," she said.

"So, you're glad you hired him, right?"

"I'd be happier if he got a haircut. That ponytail of his is hardly professional."

"Well, I can't see that happening anytime soon. I think he'll be one of those guys who still sports one in his eighties, except it will be gray by then."

"Speaking of gray hair, you're lucky to have Melvin on your boat," Nancy said. "He's very experienced. A real old salt. You know, he grew up sailing in the Bahamas. When he moved to Coconut Cove, he became a regular regatta participant, winning many years in a row."

Although Melvin Rolle had been our neighbor when we had a cottage on the beach, we had really gotten to know him because he owned the local boating supply store—Melvin's Marine Emporium—a place at which we spent a lot of time and money.

She stared out the window for a moment. "When his wife passed away, he stopped sailing. Said it reminded him too much of her," she said softly. "It's great that you're getting him back out on the water." She smiled. "It will actually be like old times—he and Ned vying against each other. We'll be on Penny's boat, you know."

"I heard about that. Is Ned up to it with his knees? Didn't he have to have them replaced? That's why he gave up racing originally, right?"

"He'll be fine. Penny has a few other people crewing as well. The young people can do the hard work while we enjoy ourselves."

"Have you told her that she isn't allowed to have red meat on her boat?"

"No, I hadn't," Nancy said. "Thanks for the reminder. I'll text her now."

Penny certainly was a brave woman to have invited Nancy to sail on her boat. By the time the regatta was over, the older woman was sure to have created a detailed manual of rules and regulations for *Pretty in Pink*.

"Make sure you keep your VHF radio on at all times, dear," Nancy said. "When your boat breaks down, you'll need to be able to call for help."

"*Marjorie Jane* is going to do fine. In fact, she's going to do great. We're planning on winning the regatta."

Nancy shook her head. "Not going to happen, dear."

"Care to place a wager?" I asked.

"What did you have in mind?"

"If we win, then you eliminate the section 72(c) from the marina contracts. I need my cheeseburgers."

She nodded. "And when *Pretty in Pink* wins, and she will, you'll keep Mrs. Moto on a leash at all times. I'm tired of seeing that mangy creature running around loose."

"Done." As I held out my hand to shake on it, I knocked over the pens.

"Be a dear and pick those up on your way out," Nancy said.

* * *

I was starting to feel a little more confident about our chances in the regatta after I successfully maneuvered *Marjorie Jane* into our slip. Yep, you read that right—I drove our boat. While I had had experience helming Penny's boat, *Pretty in Pink*, during sailing lessons, I had never driven ours. It's quite a different experience at the wheel of your own boat, especially when you're doing it in close quarters and with an audience.

There were a few bozos in the crowd making jokes about women drivers, but Scooter shut them up by saying, "You're just jealous that you don't have a talented wife like I do." Then he looked at me and said, "You're doing great, my little stegosaurus."

As I turned the wheel to angle the boat into our slip, the wind picked up, causing our stern to push out toward a very expensive-looking boat. The owner was on his deck, holding a boat hook, ready to fend us off if we came too near. I gulped, trying to remember if I had renewed our insurance policy. Somehow, I managed to steer us away from the other boat and into our spot with inches to spare.

"I'm going to need a lot of chocolate to recover from that

experience," I muttered as I ran my fingers through my hair.

Penny was standing on the dock waiting for us. "Good job, Mollie! You remembered everything I taught you."

"Very impressive," Ben said, doing a fist pump in the air.

Scooter threw both of them lines, then jumped off the boat to help tie *Marjorie Jane* off.

After turning off the engine, I let out a deep breath. I heard Mrs. Moto meowing down below. "It's okay. You can come up now. We're safe and sound." She ran up the ladder that led from the main cabin up to the cockpit, then leaped into my arms and rubbed her face against mine. "Is that your way of saying congratulations, or do you just want a treat?"

"Can you give us a hand with the fenders?" Scooter asked. "We don't want to get *Marjorie Jane's* new paint job scuffed."

"Guess treats will have to wait," I said as I set the calico down on a cushion.

After getting the fenders sorted, I joined the three of them on the dock. "I still can't believe I pulled that off."

"I had faith in you," Penny said. "Remember how you steered *Pretty in Pink* up to the fuel dock last week?"

"Yeah, but that was easier because no one was heckling me," I said.

"You had hecklers? What happened?" Ben asked.

"There were some idiots making comments about women drivers," Scooter said.

"I still get those," Penny said. "Even though I'm a sailing instructor, a licensed boat captain, and a boat broker. Some guys just can't believe a woman can be a competent boater."

"Heck, my incredible wife has more experience than me," Scooter said. "She's the one who fixed the engine."

I shrugged modestly, although I was secretly pleased at the recognition. "That's just because you're too busy with your job."

"Admit it," Ben said to me. "You kind of enjoy working on the boat."

"Sometimes, but other times, it's not a lot of fun. Definitely not fun when you've got grease and oil all over you."

Penny clapped her hands together. "Come on, we better hurry up. You don't want to be late."

"Late for what?" I asked.

"It's a surprise," she said.

I raised my eyebrows. "Oh, sure, like this morning's surprise."

"No really, I think you're going to like this one," she said.

"Do you know anything about this?" I asked Scooter.

"Nope, but I hope it involves food," he said. "I'm starved."

"It does," Penny said. "Ned's got the grill fired up."

"Hopefully, there's no red meat," I said.

"Huh?" Penny said. "Since when did you start watching what you eat?"

"Has Nancy made you guys sign a new contract by any chance?" I asked.

"She mentioned something about it to me," Ben said.

Penny shook her head. "I haven't heard anything about it."

"Well, once you see it, then you'll know what I'm talking about. In fact, you might want to check your phone, Penny. I think she texted you about dietary requirements during the regatta."

"Enough talk," Ben said. "Let's go eat."

"Let me grab my camera first," Scooter said as he hopped back on the boat.

After he took some footage of *Marjorie Jane* bobbing in her slip with Mrs. Moto posing on the bow, we all walked to the patio. When we got there, I noticed a large banner tied between two of the palm trees that read, "Happy Splash Day!"

"Is that for us?" I asked.

Penny smiled. "Uh-huh. Surprise!"

As I went to give her a hug, she said, "It's Anabel Dalton you should be thanking. She's the one who arranged everything." She pointed over at the grill where a red-haired woman wearing a long embroidered skirt and a peasant blouse was talking with Nancy. As I walked over to them, I heard my friend insisting that the patties she wanted to cook were vegetarian, not beef.

"Can you prove it?" Nancy asked.

Anabel pointed at the trashcan. "The box is in there."

Nancy stared at the garbage, then looked back at Anabel. After a brief impasse, Anabel grabbed a napkin from the table to protect her hand, reached into the trash, and pulled the box out. She held it out in front of the older woman.

"I don't have my reading glasses," Nancy said.

"Fine, I'll read the ingredients list to you," she said. When she mentioned rutabaga, I grimaced. I certainly wouldn't be eating one of those veggie burgers.

Nancy sniffed. "They sound okay, but I'd feel more comfortable if I could read it myself. Why don't you wait here while I get my glasses?"

Anabel tossed the box back into the trashcan, then squealed with delight when she saw me. "You're here! I wanted to watch you dock, but I needed to get things set up for the party."

"I can't believe you did this for us," I said.

"I may not be a boater, but I know how important splashing your boat was to the two of you. You deserve to celebrate. Everyone else thinks so too."

I smiled as I looked around the patio. Despite the relatively short amount of time we had lived in Coconut Cove, we had made some really good friends in the community. When I reflected back to my time living in a big city, I realized how much easier it was to get to know people in a small town and build meaningful relationships.

I gave her a hug. "You're such a great friend."

Mrs. Moto reached up with her front paws on my legs, letting us know that she wanted a cuddle as well. As Anabel picked the calico up, I noticed her two Yorkshire terriers were missing. "Where are Frick and Frack? Are they with their father?"

Anabel and her ex-husband, Coconut Cove's chief of police, shared joint custody of their dogs. I could never keep track of who had them on what days.

"Tiny is on his way with them," Anabel said.

I snorted at the mention of Chief Dalton's nickname, a nickname that only Anabel dared used. The rest of us were too intimidated by his gruff manner, not to mention his bushy eyebrows.

"He said he wouldn't miss this party for the world," Anabel said as she scratched Mrs. Moto behind the ears before setting her down.

I gave her a look. "Did he really say that?"

"Well, not in so many words."

"It's okay, you can admit it. The chief isn't exactly my biggest fan."

"Well ... he doesn't like people interfering in police business."

"I don't interfere. I investigate. Big difference."

"What's this about investigating?" a familiar voice asked.

I spun around and saw a burly man holding two squirming Yorkies. He set them on the ground, then Anabel greeted the over-excited dogs. As she took turns petting each of them on their heads, Mrs. Moto barreled her way in, demanding equal attention.

"Why don't the three of you go play together?" she suggested as she unclipped the dogs' leashes.

"Anabel," the chief said sternly. "What would people think if they saw that my dogs weren't on their leashes?"

"Tell you what, why don't you go check and see if Ned has everything he needs for the barbecue? That way you'll have plausible deniability," Anabel said.

He gave her an expression that on anyone else would be a frown. But I could tell from the way his lips twitched that he was amused by his ex-wife. I wondered if their romance had rekindled. They seemed to have been spending a lot of time together as of late, even without their dogs in tow.

"Come and get it," Ned called out from the barbecue before the chief could go over to assist.

Not surprisingly, the first to heed his call were the furry creatures, hoping for scraps to fall on the ground as people piled food on their plates.

"Shoo, you mangy beasts," Nancy said as she chased them off. "If you don't have opposable thumbs and aren't able to use utensils, then you'll have to stick with pet food."

The animals ignored her decree. They were actually smarter than humans in many ways. If I didn't have thumbs, I'd probably struggle to feed myself. These creatures managed to get multiple meals and snacks throughout the day without lifting a finger or using a can opener.

I grabbed a couple of pieces of chicken, potato salad, and baked beans, then joined Scooter at one of the tables. As he picked up his burger, I said, "You realize that isn't beef, right?"

"Of course it is. Ned's outdone himself tonight," he said after taking a bite. "This is really juicy."

"No, it's not. It's one of those fake burgers. Made out of beets and rutabagas."

Scooter gently set the burger back on his plate. "Did you say rutabagas?"

"Uh-huh."

"Are you going to eat both of those pieces of chicken?" Scooter asked hopefully.

I pulled my dish away. "Go grab your own."

Scooter placed his veggie burger on the ground. "Maybe the critters will enjoy this."

Mrs. Moto turned up her nose, but Frick and Frack were less discerning, gobbling it down in seconds. After the dogs had finished, the three of them ran around the patio playing chase. They darted under tables, between people's legs, and then straight into a woman who had set up an easel on the boardwalk.

She yelped as her easel and art supplies crashed to the ground. One of the Yorkies stepped on a tube of acrylic paint, squeezing green paint all over his paw, while Mrs. Moto batted a brush back and forth.

Both Anabel and I rushed over to apologize for our wayward pets.

"I'm so sorry," I said, shooing the cat and dogs away, before helping the woman to her feet.

"Watch out for my arm," the woman said. She winced as she rubbed the brace around her right wrist. "My carpal tendonitis is acting up."

"Oh, my goodness, Victoria. I can't believe this happened," Anabel said. "Maybe Tiny was right and I should have had the dogs on their leashes."

While I propped Victoria's easel back up and gathered the brushes and paint tubes, Anabel introduced us. "Mollie is the friend I was telling you about. The one who lives on a sailboat. And Victoria is a local artist. She's going to the Destiny Key retreat with me this weekend."

"I don't know if I'm going to go," Victoria said, as she adjusted a scarf tied over her long brown hair.

"Why's that?" Anabel asked.

"I can barely hold a paintbrush, let alone a pencil." She held up her right arm. "I have to wear this brace constantly. I've been trying to use my left hand more, but I'm starting to develop tendonitis in that one too. It's pretty much useless. What's the point of going when I can't do anything?"

"To hang out with me," Anabel said with a gentle smile. "Even if you can't paint or draw, you'll still have a nice time relaxing and having long conversations about art with everyone else."

Victoria's phone beeped. As she checked her text message,

her eyes started to well up. "I can't believe he would do this," she said in a soft voice.

"Do what?" Anabel asked.

"The guy I'm seeing just broke up with me."

"He did it by text?" I asked.

Tears cascaded down her face. "Yes."

Anabel pulled a tissue out of her skirt pocket and handed it to Victoria. "I didn't know you were seeing anyone."

"He wanted to keep it a secret," Victoria replied as she dabbed her eyes.

"Why? Does he have something to hide? Is he married?" I blurted out.

Victoria shook her head. "No, he was married, but he's divorced now. He's well known though, and he thought it would be better if we kept things quiet, at least for now."

"Well, the retreat is exactly what you need," Anabel said. "It will help you keep your mind off of this."

Chief Dalton walked up to us. "Everything okay here?" he asked as he looked at the green paw prints on the patio.

Scooter was standing next to him, holding a can of beer. "We thought we'd wander over and check on you ladies."

"No, everything is not okay," Victoria snapped. "First, my paintings at the gallery were ruined, my wrists are killing me, and now my boyfriend just dumped me."

"Your paintings were ruined?" Anabel asked. "What happened to them?"

"Someone sneaked into the storage room yesterday and slashed all of them. I had worked on those for months. I was getting ready to exhibit them in August. Now what am I supposed to do?"

Anabel put her arm around the distraught woman. "Tiny can help. He'll file a police report and then find out who did it."

The chief raised both of his bushy eyebrows. "Was this the incident that took place at the Coconut Creations gallery?"

Victoria nodded.

"A report was already filed," the chief said.

"By who?" Anabel asked.

"By Gregor Smirnov, the owner of the gallery," the chief said.

"That's good," Anabel said. "Have you found who did it yet? How's the investigation going?"

"It's not quite that simple." The chief looked at Victoria. "Perhaps we should discuss this privately, ma'am."

Victoria grabbed Anabel's hand. "No, I'd rather hear what you have to say with my friend to support me."

"I really think we should do this privately," Chief Dalton reiterated.

"No, please. Go ahead. I'm fine."

"Just spill it," Anabel said.

The chief looked at his ex-wife, then at Victoria. "Fine. When Mr. Smirnov phoned to report the incident, he said that you destroyed your paintings."

Victoria gasped. "Why would I destroy my own paintings?"

"He said you were very upset," the chief said.

"Of course I was upset," Victoria said, gripping Anabel's hand tightly. "Someone ruined my paintings."

"He mentioned that you're being treated by a psychiatrist. Is that true?"

Victoria gave a slight nod.

"He thought that perhaps you had stopped taking your medication, and that's why you acted out the way you did."

"No, that's not true," she whispered.

The chief leaned forward and said gently, "Mr. Smirnov is genuinely concerned about your mental well-being." He took a deep breath, then added, "And he's worried that you may be a danger to yourself, as well as others."

CHAPTER 3
OPPOSABLE THUMBS

When I woke up on Friday morning, I stretched my arms over my head then groaned.

Scooter poked his head through the doorway. "You okay?"

"I didn't sleep well last night," I said.

"More weird dreams?"

"Yes, about what Chief Dalton said about Victoria at our splash party." It had been two days but I couldn't stop thinking about it. It had been running through my head over and over. "Do you really think she could be a danger to herself or others?" I asked.

"I don't know," he said. "But it sounds like she's getting help from her doctor."

I groaned again as I shifted my position. "Speaking of doctors, I think I pulled a muscle in my neck." I propped myself up in bed, gingerly adjusting the pillows behind my head. "Remind me again why I was elected to fix our marine toilet."

We had spent the previous day getting *Marjorie Jane* ready

for the regatta. When we checked the final item off our list at seven in the evening, Scooter poured celebratory gin and tonics, while I went to wash my hands. That's when I discovered that we had a plumbing issue. I'll spare you the details. Suffice it to say that it was seriously gross.

He smiled. "It's because you're tinier than me. There's no way I would have been able to fit in the locker where the holding tank and hoses are located."

"It sucks being short." I looked over at Mrs. Moto who was nestled next to me. "You're smaller than I am. Why didn't we send you down there to repair it?"

The calico meowed, then rolled over on her back, extended her front legs and pressed her paws against my arm.

"You're not going to go with that old 'I don't have opposable thumbs' excuse again, are you?" I asked her. "Your lack of thumbs certainly doesn't get in the way when you're prying cabinet doors open and knocking your cat treats onto the floor. I'm sure you could have figured out how to use a screwdriver with one hand, grip a bracket with the other, trying not to drop the nuts and bolts, all while holding a flashlight in your mouth so you could see."

Mrs. Moto blinked her green eyes slowly at me and kneaded my arm.

"Yes, I know. You have superior night vision. You wouldn't have needed the flashlight. But you're tiny. You would have fit in that cramped space easily. I clean your litter box every day, so I think it's only fair that you fix the marine toilet next time it breaks." I squeezed one of her paws. "Deal?"

She responded by pulling her paw away, leaping across me, and running out of the cabin.

Scooter chuckled. "I don't think she liked that deal."

"I knew she was a smart cat." I turned my head from side to side, trying to get the muscles to unkink. "Any chance of some coffee?"

"It's brewing," he said. There was a tapping sound on our

hull. "You better hurry up. That'll be Melvin and Ben."

I sat up. "Is it that time already?"

"Yep. The regatta starts in a couple of hours." He rubbed the back of my neck. "Are you still up for it? Yesterday, you were talking about all the things that could go wrong."

"I think I let Nancy get into my head with all her talk about how inexperienced we are." I took a deep breath. "But I'm definitely up for the challenge. I want to prove her wrong." I turned and looked at Scooter. "What about you? Are you feeling okay about everything?"

He nodded. "I am." He held out his hand. "No matter what happens, we're not going to forget that we're a team and that we can do anything together. Deal?"

I put my hand in his and squeezed it. "Deal."

* * *

The regatta kicked off without a hitch. Ned gave a safety briefing at the marina patio, then all the boats headed to Sunshine Bay where they jockeyed for position at the starting line. When the race marshal sounded the starting horn, *Marjorie Jane* briefly took the lead before slipping behind *Pretty in Pink*. I was at the helm of the boat, the guys were managing the sails, and Mrs. Moto was perched on a cushion complaining about the fact that she was confined to the cockpit and had to wear a life jacket and tether.

"Turn a little to your port," Melvin said to me. "That's it. See how the sail is filled out now? You want to keep an eye on any little shifts in the wind and adjust your heading as needed. Okay, now just a hair to starboard."

"We need to get ahead of *Pretty in Pink*," I said as I turned the steering wheel to the right. "I don't want Nancy to beat us to Destiny Key."

The Bahamian man leaned back and smiled. "Don't worry. There's still plenty of time to catch up to her."

Ben was perched next to me. "Even if we don't win this one, there are still three other races to go. One tomorrow and one on Sunday while we're at Destiny Key, and then the race back to Coconut Cove on Monday. There's no guarantee that whoever wins today's race will be the overall regatta champion. Anything can happen."

"It looks like we'll be on this tack for a while," Scooter said. "Anyone want a drink while we have a chance to relax? We've got sodas and lemonade. There are also some brownies from the Sugar Shack."

"Are you the galley wench?" Ben laughed. "Mollie is at the helm steering the boat while you're fixing snacks."

"Wench? I'm not really sure that term works for guys," Scooter said. "How about first mate instead?"

"Really?" Ben asked. "I'd have assumed you would be the captain of *Marjorie Jane* and Mollie would be first mate."

"Why's that?" Scooter asked as he passed a cola to Melvin.

Ben cocked his head to one side. "I don't know. Aren't the guys usually the captains of boats? If you walked into the Tipsy Pirate wearing a pink t-shirt that said 'First Mate,' I think some of the old salts would give you a hard time."

Scooter chuckled. "Yeah, I can imagine what some of those old geezers would say."

Melvin took a sip of his soda before saying, "Speaking as an old geezer myself, I don't think it matters whether the captain is a man or a woman. As my dear departed Velma would say, 'Only weak men are scared by strong women.' Looks like Mollie has everything under control. Maybe she should be the one wearing the captain's hat."

I gripped the steering wheel tightly. "Me? Captain? I don't think so. That's a lot of responsibility."

"It is," Melvin agreed. "The captain has to make all the decisions and is responsible for the safety of his crew." He smiled at me and added, "Or *her* crew."

"Scooter would be so much better at that than me," I said.

"He makes decisions every day at work. Big decisions. The biggest decision I made all week was whether to have a salted caramel latte or a mocha."

"I'm not sure I want to be captain either," Scooter said as he handed a tray of brownies and napkins to Ben. "Mollie has been the one taking sailing lessons. She's a heck of a lot more competent than I am."

"Me?" I said. "Remember how Ned was talking about the weather forecast at the safety briefing? I couldn't make heads or tails of what he was saying. When he mentioned 'isobars,' all I could think of was one of those ice bars they have in Scandinavia where you wear parkas while drinking vodka shots."

Scooter chuckled. "He wasn't talking booze. It refers to atmospheric pressure."

"See? You knew that. If I was the captain, I'd probably sail us into the middle of a hurricane."

"Relax," Melvin said. "The two of you have time to figure it all out. Maybe you could be co-captains. Some couples do that. Talk about it over the weekend. Chat with other couples about what they do. There's no right or wrong answer."

"Well, one of us should at least figure out how to tell if a hurricane is headed our way," I said.

Ben scoffed as he grabbed a brownie. "Nah. You don't need to worry about that. It's way too early in the summer for a hurricane."

Melvin shook his head. "Hurricane season officially started at the beginning of June."

"Yeah, but it's only July second today."

"Don't underestimate the power of Mother Nature and when she'll decide to unleash it," Melvin said. "You've lived in Florida long enough to know what kind of damage she can cause." He took a deep breath. "I've personally seen the devastation hurricanes can leave in their wake. I've lost friends and family to one before."

"I didn't know that," I said.

Melvin twisted his wedding band while he stared out at the water. "It's not something I like to talk about."

Mrs. Moto stirred in the corner of the cockpit where she had been taking a nap. Sensing a human in need of comfort, she crawled into the older man's lap, reached up and nuzzled his face. "Now what about you, kitty-cat?" he said with a smile. "What's your title on this boat?"

Ben laughed. "That's easy. Admiral. She outranks everyone else, including the captain."

"That sounds about right," Scooter said. "She makes sure her galley wenches open up cans of cat food on a regular schedule."

Ben leaned over and scratched the admiral's head. "Maybe I should get a cat. It gets lonely living on a boat by yourself."

"I thought you were seeing someone," I said. Ben didn't exactly have a lot of luck in the ladies' department, which was a shame as he was such a sweet guy.

"She broke it off after the second date," he said, his shoulders dropping.

"That's too bad," I said.

"But there's another girl I'm thinking of asking out." His expression brightened. "She'll be at the artists' retreat. Maybe we'll run into each other."

"It's a pretty big island and we'll be at anchor," Scooter said. "I don't think it will be that easy to run into her."

"Do we know her?" I asked.

"Uh-huh. Sawyer Nichols. You've seen her when our band plays at the Tipsy Pirate. She's the singer."

"Oh, yeah," I said. "She's the girl that lives in a van."

"Yep. I've known her since high school. That's one of the reasons I think we'd be a great match. We're already good friends."

"That's an important thing in a relationship," Melvin said.

"And because she's used to living in small spaces, she'll be right at home living on a sailboat. In fact, it will seem spacious after living in a van."

"Aren't you getting a little ahead of yourself?" I asked. "Maybe you should go on a date first before you think about her moving onto your boat."

"She's a real outdoorsy kind of girl," Ben said, ignoring my comment. "She used to go camping and hunting with her dad so she's comfortable roughing it."

"What does she hunt?" Scooter asked.

"Mostly wild pigs," Ben said.

"Wow," I said. "That sounds scary."

"Nah, nothing scares her. She knows how to handle herself. She's an expert marksman."

"And she's an artist as well," Melvin said. "She sounds like a very talented young lady."

"She is," Ben said. "She went to art school in New York City before moving back to town when her dad got sick. She had been hoping to exhibit her work at the Coconut Creations gallery, but then it fell through."

"Oh, that's interesting," I said. "I wonder what Victoria would say about that given there's no love lost between her and the owner of the gallery."

Ben rubbed his chin. "Is Victoria the woman whose paintings were destroyed?"

I nodded.

"Sawyer told me about it. There are a lot of rumors going around in the art community about what happened," Ben said.

"What kind of rumors?" I asked.

Ben scratched his head. "I can't remember exactly what she said. But that's a good reason for me to try to track her down. I can get all the gossip." He grinned. "And ask her out."

* * *

"Oh, I'm stuffed," I collapsed next to Scooter, wishing my shorts had an elastic waistband. We were lying on a blanket on the public beach on Destiny Key. While we hadn't won the race to the island—*Pretty in Pink* claimed that honor—we did come in a respectable third place.

After all the boats had been safely anchored, everyone took their dinghies to shore for a barbecue. I had done my best to sample all the dishes everyone brought to share. Well, not all of them. I politely declined when Nancy offered me a low-fat Brussels sprouts and tofu rice dish. I noticed that Ned turned up his nose at it as well and went off in search of an all-beef hot dog.

"You did have a lot of brownies," Scooter said. "Not only did you eat two on the boat, you had, what three ... four ... after we got here? I wouldn't be surprised if you got a stomachache."

"It would be worth it," I said. "Did you try the ones Penny brought? The cream cheese swirl was amazing."

Melvin plopped down next to me, put his hand on his stomach, and groaned.

"Too many brownies?" Scooter asked.

"No, I didn't have any. Ever since my last doctor's appointment, I've tried to cut down on sugar. The doc said that I'm pre-diabetic."

"I wondered why you didn't have any aboard *Marjorie Jane* earlier," I said. "Impressive willpower."

"Well, I did have that soda, which I shouldn't have had. It's hard to remember what you can and can't eat. If only Velma were here, she would keep it all straight for me. She used to do most of the cooking." He took off his hat and wiped his forehead with a napkin. "Did you folks ever try that Rutamentals diet? I wonder if that would be a good solution."

My eyes grew wide. "I wouldn't if I were you. Someone we know ended up in the hospital with intestinal problems from eating too many rutabagas. She thought she had been poisoned." I looked at Melvin. "You were away when it was all the rage, weren't you?"

"Yes, back visiting family in the Bahamas." Melvin looked uncomfortable as he shifted his position.

"Are you okay?" Scooter asked.

"Just some indigestion. I'll be fine."

"I don't know. Maybe we should head back now," Scooter said.

"No, I don't want to be a bother. Besides, you and Ben wanted to play in the beach volleyball match."

"It's not a problem," Scooter said. "They'll be playing again tomorrow."

Melvin pointed at a couple stowing a cooler and a tote bag in their dinghy. "Maybe I can hitch a ride with them. Then the three of you—" Mrs. Moto yowled. "Sorry," he said giving the cat a mock salute. "The three of you and the admiral can come back when you're ready."

After Melvin left, Ben and Scooter joined the volleyball match. The idea of running around in the heat chasing after a ball didn't appeal to me, so Mrs. Moto and I sat in the shade and chatted with some of the other regatta participants about the hierarchy on their boats.

A couple of the ladies told me that they held the title of admiral. One of them was even wearing a t-shirt that said, "He may be the captain, but I'm the admiral." They were both tickled to learn that Mrs. Moto was also an admiral and took turns rubbing her belly. Another woman said that it had been her idea to buy a sailboat and she was more experienced than her boyfriend, so she was the captain on board.

A young couple sitting next to me was in the same situation as Scooter and I. They hadn't talked about who was in charge on their boat before, but it was clear from their discussion that each of them thought they should be the captain, not the other. As their bickering began to escalate into a heated argument, Mrs. Moto and I slipped away to congratulate Ben and Scooter on winning the volleyball match.

"Well, should we head back to *Marjorie Jane*?" Scooter asked.

We waved goodbye to the stragglers and walked back to where we had left our dinghy. When we arrived earlier in the afternoon, it had been high tide. Now that we were ready to leave, the tide had changed. That meant that where we parked our dinghy was now a long way away from the water. I didn't envy the guys as they carried the dinghy down the beach. It wasn't light, especially with a large outboard motor mounted on the stern, and the sharp rocks they had to walk across caused Scooter to wince in pain. Thankfully, he didn't cut his feet. If he had seen blood in the water, he might have fainted and then that would have made two heavy things to carry—the dinghy and my husband.

While they were carried the dinghy, I put Mrs. Moto's life jacket back on her. She was not pleased, to say the least. I think it might have been the bulk it added to her frame that she despised. You know what they say about the camera adding ten pounds. Even cats worry about that sort of thing.

I finally managed to fasten the straps underneath her stomach, then picked the admiral up and set her in the dinghy. She tried unsuccessfully to pry open the clasps by rubbing against the oars, then the gas tank, and finally the stern anchor.

Ben climbed into the dinghy, scooped up the cat, sat on the seat near the bow, and put her on his lap. "You'll have a better view from up here," he told her.

After helping me on board, Scooter pushed the dinghy out into the water, then hopped in. He pulled the starter cord, expecting the engine to roar to life. It didn't. He tried again and nothing happened. After the third try, he said to me, "I think it's busted. Remember that list you started of everything we need to fix? Better add the outboard motor to it."

"Hopefully, it's an easy fix," I said.

Scooter put his hand over his eyes and looked at where *Marjorie Jane* was anchored. "It's going to be a long row back."

"Um, guys," Ben said. "Did you remember to put the kill switch on before you tried to start it?"

Scooter looked at his wrist. He was wearing a red-coiled plastic band that had a small black key attached. "Oops."

"I know they're a pain," Ben said. "But they can save your life. If you ever fall overboard, because the key is attached to you, it will pop out and cut the engine off. I had a buddy get his back all torn up when he was run over by an engine propeller. You don't want that happening to you."

"Kill switch," I said. "That's a pretty gruesome name."

Scooter inserted the key. "Yeah. No more talk about people getting maimed or killed. The regatta is supposed to be fun."

"Before you start it up, I have an idea," Ben said. "You guys want to learn more about living on a sailboat and what the cruising lifestyle is like, right?"

"Sure," Scooter said.

"Well, one thing that cruisers do is go exploring on their dinghies. See that inlet there?" He pointed at a small cut at the end of the public beach. "If you go through there and make your way through the mangroves, it takes you to the most beautiful cove you've ever seen. It's really shallow, and the entrance is narrow, so you can't take a sailboat in. Want to check it out?"

"Hmm. That cove wouldn't happen to be where the artists' retreat is at, would it?"

Ben smiled. "Maybe."

"Any chance you're hoping to see Sawyer?" I asked.

"Never crossed my mind."

"Uh-huh."

"Well, you're the one who wanted to know all the art gallery gossip," Ben said. "She's got the scoop."

Mrs. Moto jumped onto the bow of the dinghy, held out her right paw, and meowed.

"See. She's pointing the way," Ben said.

Scooter chuckled. "Fine. We can check it out for a bit, but then we're heading back. Agreed?" He pulled the cord, and the engine roared to life.

After entering the inlet, Scooter steered us through the mangroves. "Is that a crocodile?" I said loudly so that I could be heard over the sound of the motor.

"Would you be happier if I told you it was a log?" Ben asked. I nodded. "Then, it's a log. So is the one with sharp teeth over there."

Eventually, the inlet opened up into the cove Ben had promised us. It really was beautiful. I wanted to sit in one of the chairs dotted about the beach and dig my toes into the white sand. There was a small dock at one end of the cove, flanked by palm trees. A large house with a veranda sat at the other end. The garden beds surrounding the house were overflowing with colorful flowers and tropical plants.

"It's called Warlock's Manor," Ben said. "All the houses on the island have funny names."

"Kind of like boats," I said.

"Do you think *Marjorie Jane* is a funny name?" Ben asked.

"It's not one I would have chosen," I said.

"Why don't you change it?" he asked.

"We're not changing it," Scooter said. "It's bad luck."

"It's only bad luck if you don't do a proper renaming ceremony," I said.

"Speaking of bad luck." Ben pointed at some dark clouds forming overhead. "Looks like we're going to get a squall."

"Let's get out of here," I said. "I don't want to get soaked. I bet the admiral doesn't want to either."

"It's just a squall. 'They come on you fast, but they leave you fast.'" Ben chucked. "Do you know what movie that's from?"

"*Captain Ron*," Scooter said. "I've seen it over twenty times."

"Twenty times too many," I muttered under my breath.

The wind started to pick up as raindrops began to fall. "Maybe we should head back," Scooter said. "We can come back tomorrow."

As he turned the tiller and pointed the dinghy back toward the mangroves, the engine died.

"Did the key come out?" Ben asked.

"No," Scooter replied. He tried to restart the engine several times, but all he was rewarded with was silence.

"I don't think it's going to start," Ben said.

By this time, we were drenched, and the wind was howling. Scooter grabbed the oars and placed them in the oarlocks. I moved toward the bow of the boat to get out of his way. He tried to row us toward the inlet, but the wind kept pushing us back.

"I can't make any headway," Scooter yelled.

"Head to Warlock's Manor," Ben suggested. "The wind will push us that way. We can wait out the storm there."

The dinghy was rocking back and forth. I gripped one of the handles on the side to keep my balance. "I thought you said this was just a squall."

"It might be more than that," Ben admitted.

I turned to look at Scooter. "Hurry," I said. "It's getting bad."

"I'm rowing as fast as I can," he said.

I patted his back. "Sorry. I know you're doing the best you can."

When I spun back around on my seat, I saw a streak of calico fur fly off the dinghy. "Stop! Mrs. Moto's fallen overboard!"

CHAPTER 4
THE SACRIFICIAL M&M'S

"Does anyone see her? Her life jacket is on the bottom of the dinghy. The little Houdini escaped from it again. What if she drowns?" I leaned over the side of the dinghy and frantically called out. "Mrs. Moto! Where are you?"

"Is that her over there?" Ben pointed at the dock. "I think I just saw something crawl out of the water."

I squinted. "I can barely see anything with this rain pouring down."

"I bet you saw that," Ben said as a chair went flying across the beach.

"Wait a minute," I said. "I think I see her. She's at the end of the dock. It's almost like she's waiting for us."

Scooter grunted as he pulled on the oars. The wind had changed direction and was pushing us backward. Scooter was struggling to keep us on course.

"We're never going to make it," I said, my voice getting squeaky. "We'll end up lost at sea and Mrs. Moto will be an orphan."

"We'll be fine, Mollie," Scooter said.

When I heard my husband say "Mollie," that's when I really began to panic. Scooter only called me by my proper name if he was worried that I was mad at him or when something was seriously wrong.

"You've got to be kidding me!" Scooter cried out.

I turned and looked at him. "What happened?"

"One of the oar locks broke. The oar slipped out of my hand." He leaned over the side of the dinghy and peered into the water. "It's down there somewhere."

"Rowing with one oar isn't going to be easy," Ben said.

My usually laid back husband snapped. "You think I don't know that?"

"Why don't I give it a shot?" Ben said. "I'm used to one-oared paddling with my kayak."

"That sounds like a good idea." I put my hand on Scooter's shoulder. "Let him take over. You're exhausted."

"Fine," Scooter said. "But let's shift positions carefully. The last thing we need is to capsize the dinghy."

I squeezed myself as close to the bow of the boat as I could while Scooter and Ben swapped places. As Ben positioned himself, his elbow knocked against the remaining oar, causing its lock to crack.

"Quick, catch it," Scooter said.

Ben twisted his body, leaning over the side of the dinghy, his hands flailing in the water.

"I think he has it," I said eagerly.

But when Ben sat up, the only thing he was holding was seaweed. "Houston, I think we have a problem," he said.

I watched in horror as the dinghy dock receded into the background while the wind continued to push us toward the mangroves.

"Grab the portable VHF radio out of that bag," Scooter said to me. "We need to call for help."

I unfastened the bag and dug around inside. I pulled out a

snorkel mask, two beach towels, Mrs. Moto's harness and leash, and a bag of M&M'S. "Um. I don't see the VHF. Are you sure you put it in here?"

"Me? I thought you packed that bag," he replied.

"I thought you did," I said.

"You're holding a bag of M&M's," he said. "That's a sure sign that you packed it."

I bit my lip. The situation was so dire that I wasn't even sure chocolate could fix our predicament. Without any way to call for help, we were doomed. Even if we did drift back out of the cove, through the mangrove, and toward the regatta boats, the rain was coming down so hard that no one would be able to see us, let alone hear our cries over the wind.

"We need a miracle," I muttered. I opened the soggy bag and popped a few chocolate morsels in my mouth. Then I remembered the stories I had heard about making offerings to the god of the sea, Poseidon, to ensure safe passage. I poured the rest of the candy morsels into the water. "Hope you like chocolate," I whispered as I watched them sink.

"Hey, the wind is changing direction," Ben said. "Look, it's pushing us toward the dock. It's a miracle."

I smiled. Everyone loved chocolate, even old Greek gods.

The dinghy drifted slowly toward shore, then a gust of wind slammed us into the dock. Scooter grabbed hold of one of the wood pilings while I tied a line to a cleat. Ben got out of the dinghy, then held out his hand to assist me. As he hoisted me onto the dock, I slipped when one of my flip-flops caught on a loose board. I grabbed Ben's arm to steady myself, then brushed my damp hair out of my eyes.

"Where did Mrs. Moto go?" I said. The downpour was so heavy that I couldn't see more than a foot or two in front of me.

"She's a smart cat," Scooter said. "She probably headed to the house. Let's go look for her there."

We made our way gingerly down the dock, holding onto

each other so that the wind wouldn't sweep us into the water. After we reached the end of the dock, we picked up the pace, running across the wet sand while dodging coconuts flying off the palm trees. Once we reached the safety of the covered veranda, I asked Ben if this was the start of a hurricane.

"I don't know what this is," he said as he pounded on the door. "I'm just glad we have shelter."

After a few moments, the door creaked open. Thomas stood there looking at us in surprise.

"Where in the world did you folks come from?" he asked.

Ben started to tell him about our adventure, but I interrupted. "Have you seen our cat?"

"A bobtailed calico?" I nodded. "She's inside. I found her out here yowling. I figured she got lost in the storm."

After I explained about our dinghy problems and how Mrs. Moto had removed her life jacket despite her lack of opposable thumbs and then swum for shore, Thomas smiled. "She sounds like a smart cookie. Maybe she's even a little psychic. She might have known what was going to happen with the oars." He took a step back. "What's wrong with me? Talking about psychic powers when you folks are dripping wet. Come on inside." After we stepped into the tiled foyer, he added. "Wait here and I'll grab some towels for you."

As he started to walk down the hallway, I said, "Do you have a VHF by any chance? Melvin, our other crew member, went back to *Marjorie Jane* earlier and he'll be wondering what happened to us."

"Sure, I've got one. Why don't I hail your boat first, then I'll be right back."

"Where is that cat?" Scooter asked. "I would have thought that when she heard our voices, she'd come running out to check on us."

"You just want to film a happy reunion. Wait a minute, is your phone okay? Did it get ruined in the storm?"

Scooter took a waterproof pouch out of one of the pockets

of his cargo shorts and pulled his cell out. "It looks fine. Hang on. I can call Melvin rather than have Thomas try to reach him with the VHF." After punching in the number and waiting for it to ring, he looked at the screen. "Nope. No service. Must be the storm."

"I hope Thomas gets through to him," I said.

After a few anxious minutes, the artist returned carrying a pile of towels. "Melvin's glad you're okay. While they can see the storm over Destiny Key, he said that the weather is perfectly calm where they are."

"How is that possible?" I asked.

"Strange things have been known to happen on this island," Thomas said. "Things people can't exactly explain. Odd weather patterns and other things."

"Like ghosts?" Ben asked.

"Well, there are some interesting legends about that," Thomas said.

"Ghosts aren't real," I said.

Ben snorted. "And all the aliens you always talk about are?"

"Sure," I said. "You really need to come to one of my FAROUT meetings one of these days."

"Remind me again what FAROUT stands for?" Ben asked.

"The Federation for Alien Research, Outreach, and UFO Tracking. We just had a really interesting presentation about the latest scientific proof of the existence of alien life."

"I'm not sure everyone would agree with you that there's real proof," Ben said.

"Scooter does."

"You do?" Ben asked Scooter.

"I, uh—" Before my husband could finish what he was going to say, a bright flash of lightning shone through the windows, followed by a loud clap of thunder.

"That sounded like it was right overhead," I said.

"It was pretty close," Thomas said. "Tell you what. You

folks look like you could use a drink. Why don't you finish toweling off, then I'll get you some dry clothes and you can join the others in the drawing room."

I startled as another clap of thunder boomed. "They're getting closer," I said.

"We'll be fine," Scooter said, putting his arm around my shoulder.

"You should be happy you're not on a sailboat," Ben said. "Masts are like lightning rods. Lots of boats in Florida get struck every year."

"That's very reassuring," I said, a tad sarcastically.

Three more thunderclaps took place in quick succession, then all of the lights in the entryway went off.

"Power's out," Thomas announced. "Let me see if I can find a flashlight. You would think it was nighttime already given how dark it is with the storm. I know there's one in the console table here somewhere. And then I'll turn on the emergency generator." We listened as he rustled through the drawers. "Ta-da!"

As he turned the flashlight on, the front door crashed open. Thomas swept the beam of light toward the entryway, illuminating a man dressed all in black leaning on a cane.

"What are you doing here, Gregor?" Thomas asked.

"I was invited," he replied. "Now, fetch me some dry clothes and a brandy."

* * *

"This is unacceptable." Gregor looked down at the white Hello Kitty t-shirt he was wearing. It was at least two sizes too small for him. I was surprised that he wasn't also complaining about the over-sized purple and orange striped pajama bottoms he had on, especially since he had to hold them up with one hand so they wouldn't fall down.

Thomas shrugged. "Sorry. That's all I had." He had loaned

all of us dry clothes and hung up our wet ones to dry. Personally, I would have preferred Gregor's t-shirt to the one I was wearing. Giraffes weren't really my thing. Something about their long necks always unnerved me.

"Give me an outfit like theirs," Gregor said, pointing at Ben and Scooter, who were wearing plain t-shirts and sweatpants. "An outfit that fits properly and doesn't have a childish cat on it."

Thomas bit back a smile. I had a feeling he might have selected Gregor's clothes with a certain sense of vengeance in mind. "It's either what you're wearing or your wet clothes. Your choice."

Gregor shuffled toward an armchair by the bay window, holding his cane in one hand and his pajama bottoms with the other. The rest of us were already sitting down in the large drawing room, sipping on brandy. Everyone except Mrs. Moto, that is. She was lapping up milk from a saucer, looking no worse for wear after her swim.

While Gregor continued to complain loudly, this time about the quality of the liquor Thomas was serving, I surveyed the room and its occupants—the participants in the artists' retreat. There were two small couches arranged parallel to each other in front of a large marble fireplace. Victoria and Anabel were sitting on one, Olivia and Sawyer on the other. Ben had perched on the armrest next to Sawyer and was whispering something in her ear while she giggled periodically. Olivia was oblivious to their conversation, focused on editing videos on her laptop.

Victoria looked warily at Gregor, then averted her eyes. I could only imagine what was going through her head. This was the man who had told Chief Dalton that she was mentally unstable and had destroyed her own paintings. Anabel squeezed Victoria's hand, then fixed a steely glare on the Russian.

"The others have explained how they ended up at

Warlock's Manor," Anabel said. "But why are you here?"

Gregor tugged at his t-shirt, trying to stretch it out, then gave up. "It is no concern of yours."

Thomas took a sip of his drink, then said, "If you're at Warlock's Manor, it certainly is my concern."

"Fine," Gregor said. "I will tell you. I went to see an art collector. A very important client. A very rich client. He wants to buy a painting from a man in Paris with whom I am acquainted. I arranged the deal."

"And earned a nice little commission in the process," Thomas said bitterly.

Gregor took a sip of a brandy and made a face. "How do you drink this swill?"

"I'm worried about Thomas' blood pressure," I whispered to Scooter. "Look how red his face is."

Thomas gulped down the rest of his brandy. "You still haven't explained why you're here. You said someone invited you."

"Did I say that?" Gregor said with a brittle smile. "Perhaps I misspoke. I had time before the return ferry. I decided to stop here for a visit beforehand."

"How did you get to the house? Do you have a car?" Scooter asked. "Maybe you can drive us to the public beach and someone from one of the other boats can send a dinghy for us."

"No, I do not have a car. I borrowed a golf cart from my client. But the road is now impassable. There is a large tree blocking the way. "

"He's telling the truth," Thomas said. "I talked to the ferry operator on the VHF. The whole island is shut down. No cell phone service, and no way on or off until the storm passes."

"And when will that be?" I asked.

Thomas shrugged. "No idea. Like I said, Destiny Key is an unusual place."

"It is late and I am exhausted," Gregor said, placing his

glass on an end table. "You may prepare a room for me now."

"You expect to stay here tonight?" Thomas asked. "After the way you've treated me?"

"This is not your house," Gregor said. "I am sure the owner would be honored to know that I stayed here."

I exchanged glances with Scooter. Did Thomas expect us to go back out in the rain as well? As if he were able to read my mind, Thomas turned to us. "I didn't mean you guys. There's a bunkhouse that you can stay in. Then we can work out in the morning how to get you back to your boat." He sighed. "You can stay there too, Gregor."

"Bunkhouse? Bunk beds?" Gregor shook his head. "No. That will not do."

"Well, we're all full up here," Thomas said. He pointed at Sawyer and Olivia. "The girls are sharing one of the larger guest rooms. Victoria and Anabel each have one of the smaller ones, and I'm in the master suite. I'm sure you don't expect any of us to give up our rooms to you."

Gregor slowly tapped his cane on the floor while he considered what Thomas said. "Fine. I shall stay with Victoria in her room."

"With Victoria?" Anabel asked, nearly spitting out her drink.

"It's okay. He can stay with me," Victoria said weakly.

"Him? Why would you let him stay with you?" Anabel asked. "Wait a minute. Is this the boyfriend you were talking about? The man who dumped you and—"

"Dump her?" Gregor protested. "I did no such thing. Tell them, my *kroshka*."

Victoria stared at the floor without saying a word while she rubbed her wrist.

"What do you think a *kroshka* is?" I whispered Scooter.

"Maybe it's Russian for stegosaurus," he replied.

"Explain to them that it was nothing," Gregor repeated.

Victoria lifted her head and sat up straight. "You *did* break up with me. I have the text to prove it."

He waved his hands in the air. "You are overreacting as usual."

"It's true. I saw the text," I said.

"It was a lovers' tiff," Gregor said to me. "She is, how you say ... high-strung. She has an artistic temperament." He looked at Victoria. "But our tiff is over now, is it not, my *kroshka*?"

Anabel rose to her feet and walked over to the side table where the crystal liquor decanters were located. "You aren't going to share her room," she said over her shoulder. "I won't stand for it."

"I don't want him to stay with us either," I whispered to Scooter.

Gregor stood, steadied himself on his cane, then slowly made his way to the couch Anabel had vacated. As he sat next to Victoria, he looked around the room. "She knows I love her." Then he gently took her hand in his and kissed it dramatically.

Victoria's face lit up as she leaned into him.

"You think one kiss is going to make up for what you did?" Anabel said, waving her glass back and forth so forcefully that brandy sloshed out of it. "You told the police that she was mentally unbalanced."

Gregor shook his head. "I did no such thing."

"Yes, you did. I should know. Tiny is my..." She struggled to find the right word to define her relationship with the police chief. "He's my ex. He told me what you said."

"I was there too when the chief filled us in," I chimed in.

"You Americans," Gregor said playfully. "Never can take a joke. I was not serious."

"People like you give the art community a bad name," Anabel said loudly. "The way you treat women is shocking. If I were you, I would think twice before walking down a dark alley alone."

Ben and Sawyer looked at each other in shock. Even Olivia looked up from her computer as Anabel's voice became more shrill. No doubt she was wishing that she had her video camera handy to record the drama.

Thomas said soothingly, "It's late. Maybe we should all turn in."

Olivia held out her glass. "How about another drink first?"

"Not for us." Gregor rose and poked his cane at Victoria's leg. "We will retire now. Come, my *kroshka.*"

Victoria stood and followed him to the doorway. As she passed Anabel, she said softly, "It's okay. You don't need to worry."

After Thomas refilled everyone's glasses, Ben said, "I don't want to crowd you guys in the bunkhouse. Why don't I sleep on one of these couches?"

"They're tiny," I said. "You wouldn't fit on them."

"It's fine, Ben," Scooter said. "Stay in the bunkhouse with the admiral and us. Speaking of, where did that cat disappear to now?"

"She's napping next to me," Olivia said, moving her computer to one side so we could see two pointed ears peeking out from underneath an afghan.

A loud crash reverberated throughout the drawing room, startling Mrs. Moto. She clawed at the blanket she was wrapped in, then tore out of the room.

Thomas looked out the bay window. "I think we lost another tree."

"I better go check on the admiral and make sure she's okay," I said.

As I followed the calico out into the hallway and started to climb the staircase, I heard Victoria and Gregor speaking on the floor above me about her destroyed paintings. She seemed to be distraught, so I paused on the landing to give them some privacy.

Okay, maybe it wasn't about giving them privacy, although

their conversation was kind of private. It was more that they didn't know I was listening. I really had Victoria's best interests at heart. Given the way Gregor had treated her, I wanted to make sure she was okay.

As I leaned against the wall, I heard Victoria ask Gregor why he told Chief Dalton that she had destroyed her own paintings.

"We do not want him poking around in things that are not his business," Gregor said. "Small-town police officers are idiots. All they are good for is giving out parking tickets."

Part of me agreed with Gregor's assessment. If it hadn't been for my invaluable investigative expertise, none of the recent murder cases in Coconut Cove would have been solved. The only way a murderer would have been caught is if she or he tried to drive out of town and was stopped for exceeding the speed limit.

"So you don't think I'm crazy?" Victoria asked.

Gregor made soothing sounds. "No. You are not crazy. You are my beautiful *kroshka*. I know that you did not destroy your paintings."

"Who do you think did it?" she asked.

"I have an idea," he said.

"Tell me," she said. "Who did this?"

"Not yet. First, I must find out more. You trust me, no? While I am here at Warlock's Manor, I will confirm my suspicions."

"You mean it was someone here on the retreat?"

"Perhaps. You are very talented. Perhaps someone was jealous of your talent. Perhaps they were jealous that you are my one and only *kroshka*. Now, wipe your tears and come to bed."

As I heard the door to Victoria's room close, I was left with two questions—what was a *kroshka* and who had ruined Victoria's paintings?

* * *

Early the next morning, I felt a sharp pain on my chest. Not the kind of pain that signals an imminent heart attack, but rather that of a very demanding feline who normally weighs a dainty eight pounds, but somehow feels more like thirty-five pounds when she's pressing her paws into you. She accompanied each stab of her paw with a shrieking yowl.

"Just stop already. I heard you the first time," I said as I pulled the covers over my head. "But it's not time for breakfast."

The sharp pain on my chest disappeared, only to be replaced by sharp pains on my neck and face as Mrs. Moto walked over me. She then settled down on the top of my pillow. I turned on my side and tightened the covers to create a protective barrier around myself.

The admiral was not to be deterred by my pathetic attempt to get some more shut-eye. In the face of my non-compliance with her wishes, she decided to carry out 'Operation Feed the Poor Starving Cat.'

First, she snaked her paw in between the sheet and the pillow and tapped me on my head. When I didn't respond, she extended her claws and tugged at my hair. I curled up in a ball and tried to ignore the fact that she was turning my already normally frizzy hair into an even bigger rat's nest.

When she became bored with that part of her campaign, she moved on to the bounce and pounce phase. As you can imagine, it involves a lot of bouncing and pouncing on the human target, especially their feet. I asked Mrs. Moto how a cat who is supposedly starving to death can find the energy to keep up this level of attack, but her only response was to chew on my toes before leaping back onto my chest.

She sat quietly for a few moments. Naturally, that made me suspicious. I peeked over the top of my covers. Her emerald green eyes bored into me. It was unnerving, almost as though she was trying to speak to me telepathically. Even though I couldn't hear her thoughts, I was pretty sure I knew what she was saying. "Hey, two-legged creature. Show me how powerful you are. Use your opposable thumbs and open up a can of Frisky Feline Ocean's Delight, pronto."

When I didn't respond (verbally or telepathically), she padded up my chest and lay down on my face. I wasn't sure this was a smart strategy on her part. Suffocating your human makes them less likely to feed you. It's hard to operate a can opener when you're suffering from oxygen deprivation.

"Just move your paw a little to the right," a voice said. "That's it. Perfect."

It was hard to make out who was speaking with all that fur pressed against my ear. I reached up and pushed Mrs. Moto to the side. As I brushed cat hair off my face, I noticed Scooter beaming at me while holding up his phone. "Don't tell me you've been filming this," I said.

"Of course, I have. I'm recording a vlog—a day in the life of Mrs. Moto."

I ran my fingers through my hair, attempting to untangle it. As I caught sight of myself in a mirror on the wall, I groaned. "You better edit out the parts with me in it. I look like a mess."

Scooter leaned down and kissed me on my forehead. "You look gorgeous." Mrs. Moto meowed loudly. "See, she agrees too."

I quickly propped my pillows behind me and sat up in bed before my pesky feline could try to settle back on my face. "Where's Ben?"

Scooter pointed at the upper bunk on the opposite side of the room. "He's still snoozing away."

"I can't believe he could sleep through all the commotion this one has been making," I said, scratching Mrs. Moto behind her ears. "What time is it?"

Scooter looked at his phone. "Around six. No wonder she's hungry."

"I'm pretty hungry too. Breakfast is at eight, but I don't think I can wait until then. Why don't I take her up to the main house? Thomas said I could feed her some of the leftover ham in the fridge. I'll see if there's something else I can snack on as well. Do you want anything?"

"Nah, I'm good. I can wait until later. I want to check out what I've shot so far."

After quickly getting ready, I opened the bunkhouse door. "Gosh, it's foggy out there. But at least it stopped raining." Mrs. Moto flew past me. "Hey, wait for me."

I could barely keep up with the calico as she ran toward the main house. She darted up on the porch, then sat on the welcome mat and pawed at the door, eager for her breakfast. As I started to turn the knob, she cocked her head to one side. Her ears flattened down and the fur on her back stood straight up.

She jumped onto the porch railing, knocking a pair of reading glasses and one of Thomas' cuff links on the ground. As I bent to pick them up, she yowled before leaping off and running toward the dinghy dock.

"What about your breakfast?" I yelled after her. "You're not the only one who's hungry. We can look at the fish later."

As I walked down the dock, taking care not to slip, I saw her standing by the cleat where our dinghy had been tied off. It was nowhere to be seen. I groaned. "Don't tell me it sank in the storm."

Mrs. Moto rubbed against my ankles while I thought about how much money it would cost to replace our dinghy. As I peered out into the fog, I could just about make out a shape bobbing in the water. Could that be our dinghy? How did it get out there?

There was a line coming up from under the dock and toward the floating object. If I was lucky, the stern anchor had fallen overboard and the end of the line nearest to me was attached to it while the other end was attached to the dinghy. If that was the case, I could try to use the anchor line to pull the dinghy back toward me.

I lay down on the dock to see if I could reach the line with my hand, but it was too far away. It probably also didn't help that Mrs. Moto climbed onto my back while I was trying to get a hold of it.

"Come on kitty, let's find something to snag the line." We walked to the end of the dock where I spotted an old rusty boat hook. That did the trick. I was able to snag the line and pull it close enough to me to be able to grab it with my hands. Then I stood and pulled what I hoped was our dinghy toward the dock.

"Wow. This dinghy is heavier than I remember," I said. "Maybe because it's full of water from the storm."

I continued to pull on the line, hand over hand until the object came into view. "It is our dinghy," I said to Mrs. Moto. Then I almost dropped the line in the water in shock. There was a reason why it was heavier than normal—Gregor was lying in it motionless, his arms and legs sprawled over the side. As I pulled the dinghy closer to the dock to tie it off, the fog cleared and I could see him clearly. So clearly that I could make out a dark red stain on the center of his Hello Kitty t-shirt. A dark red stain the color of blood.

"I think he's dead," I said.

Mrs. Moto meowed in agreement.

CHAPTER 5
ANNOYING SEAGULLS

After taking a deep breath to calm myself, I finished securing the dinghy to the dock. As I leaned over and felt for a pulse, I confirmed my suspicion—Gregor was dead. The wound on his chest sent chills down my spine. This wasn't an accidental death. He had been stabbed.

"Let's go get help, Mrs. Moto," I said.

The calico yowled, then raced up the beach toward the house. I followed at a slower pace, pausing occasionally to stop and look back at the dock. Who could have killed Gregor, and why?

As I neared Warlock's Manor, Scooter and Thomas were standing on the veranda, the agitated cat running circles around them and meowing loudly. Scooter was still wearing the t-shirt and sweatpants he had borrowed the previous night. Thomas was already dressed for the day in one of his eccentric outfits—a dark blue button-down shirt, a tie with a pineapple print on it, a canary yellow vest, hot pink trousers with a yellow pinstripe, and his customary flip-flops.

"How was your walk?" Thomas asked. He looked up at the sky. "Now that the storm has passed, it looks like it's going to be a beautiful day."

I frowned. "It wasn't exactly a walk."

"Everything okay?" Scooter asked before giving me a quick kiss on the cheek. "You seem lost in thought."

"No, everything's not—" I started to say.

"Hang on a minute," Scooter said. He scooped Mrs. Moto up and held her in his arms. "What's gotten into you? You keep screaming like you haven't been fed in weeks." He turned to me. "You did feed her, right?"

"Actually, I didn't have a chance."

"We'll have to remedy that, won't we my little admiral?" Scooter cooed. Mrs. Moto squirmed out of his arms and ran toward the dock. "The kitchen's back here," he yelled after her.

"Maybe she doesn't like ham," Thomas suggested.

"No, she loves ham," Scooter said. "I don't know what's gotten into her. It's like she's on some sort of mission."

"She is," I said.

"Huh? What kind of mission?" Scooter asked.

"Well, I'm not quite sure how to put this," I said.

Scooter pushed his glasses up on his nose. "What's going on?"

I took a deep breath. "Gregor is dead."

Thomas gasped. "Dead?"

"Yes," I said. "Dead in our dinghy."

"But...but how?" Thomas asked. "Was it a heart attack?"

"I don't think so."

"A stroke?"

I shook my head.

Thomas continued listing potential causes of death for men over the age of sixty. I suspected that he had a lot of medical sites bookmarked on his computer.

When he ran out of possible explanations related to

natural death, Scooter asked, "Why do I have a bad feeling about this?"

I pointed at the porch swing. "You might want to sit down."

"I think I know where this going," Scooter said as he sat at one end of the swing.

Thomas continued to stand, his gaze darting back and forth between Scooter and me.

"I think Gregor was murdered." I paused to gauge Thomas' reaction. He had been pretty vocal in his dislike of Gregor. How did he feel about his demise? Then I had a chilling thought—what if Thomas had been the one to stab him?

"Are you sure it wasn't a heart attack or stroke?" the artist asked in a quiet voice.

"I'm sure," I said.

"How sure?" Thomas asked.

I was about to tell him about the blood, when I noticed Scooter's ashen face. A description of how Gregor had died was going to be too much for him to handle. Normally, in situations like this, I would give him some chocolate, but all my M&M'S were at the bottom of the sea.

"Maybe I should show you instead," I suggested to Thomas. "Scooter, why don't you wait here?"

"Okay," both of them said at the same time. Scooter looked relieved. Thomas looked apprehensive.

As we walked down the beach, I asked, "Are you sure you want to see this?"

Thomas paused and straightened his shoulders. "I'll be fine. I've taken first aid courses before."

"Uh, this isn't quite the same thing," I said.

He nodded slowly, then continued toward the dock. Mrs. Moto met us halfway. She gave a plaintive meow before escorting us the rest of the way.

After Thomas looked at the body, he said, "You're right. This wasn't a heart attack."

I put my hand on his arm. "Maybe we should go back and call the authorities."

Thomas ignored me, continuing to stare at Gregor, his expression alternating between shock and something that almost looked like relief.

"Let's go back to the house, okay?" I said. "Does Destiny Key have its own police force?"

Thomas tore his gaze away from the dinghy. "Um, yeah. They do. The chief of police is actually Michael's cousin." I looked at him blankly. "Michael is the guy who owns Warlock's Manor. I'll give the chief a call." He reached into his pocket and pulled his cell phone out. "Cell service is still down. I'll have to try him on the VHF."

As we walked back down the beach, I asked if he knew if Gregor had any relatives in the area.

Thomas shrugged. "I have no idea. My only interactions with him had to do with the art world."

"It seemed like there was some bad blood between the two of you."

He gave a wry laugh. "That's putting it mildly." Then he gave me an appraising look. "Wait, you don't think I had anything to do with this, do you?"

I held my hands up. "No, I'm not saying that. I'm just curious about him is all. No one seemed happy to see him when he arrived last night. Except maybe Victoria, and I'm not even sure about that."

"I don't know why she put up with him," Thomas said bitterly. "He was emotionally abusive to her."

"So you knew they were seeing each other?" I asked.

"Yes. She confided in me once after they'd had a big fight. But she begged me to keep it to myself. I shouldn't have. I've known men like that before. I should have made sure she got help." He shoved his hands in his pockets. "But at least she's free of him now."

"Speaking of Victoria," I said, pointing at the house. She

was standing on the veranda with Anabel. Both of the women were holding mugs, reminding me that I hadn't had my morning coffee. With all the adrenaline coursing through my body as a result of finding Gregor, I hadn't needed my usual caffeine fix.

"I better go break the news to her," Thomas said. "Then I'll try to get a hold of Chief Tyler."

I sat on the porch swing next to Scooter. The color had returned to his face. Mrs. Moto was curled up in his lap, purring loudly as he stroked her.

"So it really is mur..." His voice trailed off. He couldn't bring himself to say 'murder' out loud.

I nodded as I reached over to scratch the calico's head. We sat in silence for a few moments watching as Thomas explained to Victoria what had happened. She collapsed into his arms, sobbing uncontrollably. Then she pulled away and rubbed her eyes.

"I need to see him," she said.

"You don't want to see him like that," Thomas said.

She flapped her hands in the air. "I need to make sure he's dead."

"Trust me. You don't want to do this," Thomas said.

Anabel grabbed Victoria's hand. "Why don't we go inside and have some more coffee?"

Victoria shook her head. "I don't want coffee. I want to see Gregor." She walked down the veranda steps shakily.

Anabel rushed over to her. "At least let me come with you," she said, putting her hand through Victoria's arm.

"Mollie, why don't you go with them?" Thomas said. "I really need to call the chief."

I rose and walked over to the two women. Victoria's face looked drawn and she was shivering despite the warmth of the sun. I put my hand through Victoria's other arm so that Anabel and I could help steady her as we walked down the beach.

When we reached the dinghy, the grieving woman inhaled sharply. She fell to her knees, mumbling Gregor's name in between sobs. Anabel tried to help her to her feet, but she shook her off.

"Why don't we give her a minute?" I suggested.

While we waited, some seagulls circled overhead. Looking at the bright sun and blue sky, it was hard to believe that there had been such a violent storm the previous night, let alone a murder.

"You ready for that coffee?" Anabel asked Victoria gently.

Victoria clasped her hands in front of her and closed her eyes as if in prayer. Then she rose to her feet. Her foot caught on the boat hook, causing her to lose her balance. I quickly grabbed her to keep her from falling in the water.

"I'm fine," she said, brushing me off. "I need a few minutes to myself. I'm going to walk along the beach."

After watching to make sure she got to the end of the dock safely, Anabel turned to me. "Do you know what she told me this morning? Gregor proposed to her last night. She was so happy. They were planning on being married at Christmastime."

"Why would she agree to marry him?" I asked. "Thomas told me that he was emotionally abusive to her."

"You got me," Anabel said. "I couldn't believe it when I realized that he was who she had been seeing. Gregor was always bragging about how he was some sort of international playboy."

I snorted. "Him?"

"He was rich. Some women find that attractive. He once showed me pictures of him with a beautiful model on his arm at an art show in New York City. Compared to that young woman, Victoria is, well..."

"Older?" I suggested.

"Let's just say that she didn't seem like his type. But maybe that's why she liked him. She might have felt good that he chose her over a younger woman."

"But that might have also made her insecure," I said. "She'd always be worried that he was going to ditch her."

"And he did the other night when he sent her that text."

"But he claimed that it was a lovers' tiff," I said.

"I wonder how many times he did that to her before," Anabel mused.

"How long had they been dating?"

"I'm not sure," Anabel said. "That's a good question. She first mentioned that she was seeing someone a few weeks ago when we were having lunch, but it might have started before then."

"If it was just a few weeks ago, that would have been a quick engagement. I didn't notice a ring on Victoria's finger."

"He didn't give her one. She said it was a spontaneous proposal, but that he promised he'd give her a ring soon. He was planning on having one designed for her by an artist in Paris. It was going to be a large ruby with emeralds on either side. From the way she described the ring, it sounded like the ruby was going to be the size of a walnut."

I looked down at my own diamond engagement ring and wedding band and smiled as I thought back to when Scooter and I had decided to get married. There was still some disagreement as to who had proposed to whom, but we both had agreed as to the type of wedding we wanted—small and slightly quirky. It did turn out that our idea of quirky differed. For some reason, Scooter drew the line at a Star Wars theme.

"Why don't we go get some coffee?" Anabel asked, interrupting my thoughts.

One of the seagulls landed in the dinghy. "Shoo," I said, tugging on the line to scare it off. "Get out of there."

That one flew away, only to be replaced by two others. I jumped up and down, waving my hands wildly to scare them off.

"I think I better stay here before this turns into some kind of Hitchcock movie," I said.

"You mean like *The Birds*?" Anabel asked.

"Uh-huh. Ned showed that at the marina last week. Gave me nightmares. The last thing we need is a gang of birds attacking us. Why don't you go back to the house and find out if Thomas got hold of the chief of police and when he'll be here?"

"Okay," she said. As she turned to leave, she looked back at Gregor, then quietly said, "Good riddance."

* * *

I'm not sure why the seagulls thought the scene of a murder was so fascinating, but every time I scared one off, more swooped down to check things out. It was time to call in reinforcements. I saw Scooter and Mrs. Moto halfway down the beach and hurried over to them.

"I need to borrow the admiral for a while," I said to Scooter.

He was kneeling on the sand videoing the calico while she chased a crab. He looked up at me. "Why's that?"

"There are some seagulls I want to introduce her to." I explained how a large crowd of them was gathering by the dinghy. "She's always been good at chasing birds away."

"Ooh. That would be a fun to film." He paused as he remembered exactly what was in the dinghy. "Wait a minute, maybe it wouldn't be that much fun."

"I'm also going to need your phone. I want to take some pictures of Gregor's, um, body."

"Not on my phone, you're not." Scooter clutched his cell close to him. "Why are you getting involved, anyway? Thomas said he was calling the police."

"I'm not getting involved. I'm just documenting the scene." I peered over my shoulder at the dock. There was a lone seagull sitting on one of the posts. "I promise not to drop your phone in the water."

"That's not what I'm worried about. I don't want pictures of a, um..." He tried to keep from saying 'dead body' out loud, but couldn't find a suitable euphemism.

"Recently departed person?" I suggested.

He nodded.

"Don't worry. I'll email the photos to me and delete them before I return it." I held out my hand. He reluctantly put the phone in it.

"Now, where did that cat go?" Scooter asked.

Hearing a splashing sound behind me, I turned to look at the water and saw the calico happily paddling along the shoreline. "Oh my gosh, she's swimming again."

"Do you think she actually likes that?" Scooter asked.

"Well, it's not like last night when she might have just been trying to escape from the dinghy. She voluntarily went in the water this time."

"That's the strangest thing. I didn't know cats liked to swim." He grabbed the phone back from me. "I've got to get this on camera. Mrs. Moto's fans are going to love this."

"Fans? She has fans?"

"Uh-huh. And a fan club. They're called the Kalico Kittens."

"How many members are there?"

"Well, just three right now," he admitted. "But once we launch the YouTube channel, it's going to explode. I'm going to set up an online shop with all sorts of merchandise with the Kalico Kittens logo on it."

The conversation reminded me of Gregor's Hello Kitty t-shirt and the need to get back to defend the dinghy from the birds. "Here kitty, kitty," I called out. "Come with mama and let's go chase some birds."

The admiral swam back to shore, shook water off her fur, then promptly plopped down on the beach and rolled over.

"Ugh. Now you have sand all over you," Scooter said.

"That's the problem with wet fur. Stuff clings to it."

As he tried to wipe her off with his hands, Anabel joined us. "The good news is that Thomas managed to get a hold of Chief Tyler," she said. "The bad news is that he doesn't know when he can get here."

"Doesn't he know there's been a murder?" I asked.

"Thomas explained it to him, but he said he has other things to deal with at the moment. Besides, the main road is still blocked, and it will be a while before it can be cleared."

"Can't he come by boat?"

"No, that isn't an option. Thomas also spoke with Melvin. Apparently Penny and he tried to come here this morning in her dinghy, but the inlet to the cove is blocked as well with storm debris. Looks like we're going to have to wait."

I put my hands on my hips and frowned.

"It's not like Gregor's going anywhere," Scooter said.

"It's the birds I'm worried about. Ready, Mrs. Moto?" She squirmed out of his arms and led the way to the dock.

"Wait for me," Anabel said. "I'll keep you company."

I smiled. "I can tell that you used to be married to a police officer. Not many people would call watching over a murder scene 'keeping company.'"

"I guess I got used to that sort of thing being married to Tiny," she said.

"He took you to crime scenes?" I asked.

"No, nothing like that, but he'd talk about his cases over dinner."

I tried to imagine the chief willingly chatting about anything, let alone his cases.

Anabel must have seen my confusion. "He didn't tell me the details, but he'd share a few things."

As we walked down the dock, she asked, "Do you really think it was murder? Is it possible it was an accident?"

"Look at his chest," I said when we reached the dinghy. "I don't think there's any way he could have accidentally stabbed himself and then fallen in there on his back. Unless you see something around here that could have done that?"

"There's a rusty nail sticking out of this post," she said. "Maybe he slipped on the dock, stumbled into the post, and the nail went into him."

"Do you see any blood on it?" I asked.

She peered at the nail. "No. But with the rain last night, it would have washed it away."

I wondered what other evidence the storm might have destroyed. "Good point. But I'm still not sure that a nail could have created that kind of wound."

She picked up the boat hook I had used earlier to snag the stern anchor line. "What about this?"

"I can see someone using it as a club, but there aren't any sharp points on it. Everything is smooth, rounded plastic and metal." Mrs. Moto meowed at the end of the dock. "Do you see something?" I asked her.

We walked over and peered in the water. The only things I could make out in the rocks surrounding the dock were some small red circular objects.

"What is that?" Anabel asked. "Blood?"

"No. I think they might be M&M'S. I wonder how long it takes for them to dissolve in water," I mused.

"You think the killer was eating candy?" she asked.

"No, those were mine. Although that might be an interesting idea—profiling criminals based on the candy they eat."

Anabel laughed. "Given how much sugar you consume, you'd be in trouble. You'd fit every profile."

I glanced at her, thinking about what she had said previously. "Are you really glad he's dead?"

She raised her eyebrows. "Huh? What do you mean?"

"Well, before you left earlier, I heard you say, 'good riddance,'"

"Of course I'm not glad he's dead." Her eyes rounded. "I

don't like the idea of anyone being killed, even someone like Gregor. I must have been thinking about Victoria when that slipped out."

"That's the type of thing you might want to keep to yourself," I said. "You never know how someone might interpret it. Or rather misinterpret it."

"You don't seriously think I killed Gregor?"

"Oh my gosh, no," I said. "I wouldn't want anyone else to think it, that's all."

"Someone who's guilty wouldn't say something like that, anyway," she said. "They'd want to throw suspicion off of themselves. They'd act upset."

We both looked at Victoria. She had rolled her pants up above her knees and was wading in the water. She had sobbed uncontrollably when she saw Gregor. Had it all been an act? Had she been trying to throw off suspicion from herself?

"Would they also pretend to be in love with the victim?" I asked. "Pretend to be engaged?"

"I know what you're thinking, but there's no way Victoria could have killed Gregor." Anabel frowned. "You're as bad as Tiny, always thinking the worst of people."

"I'm sorry. I know she's your friend. Scooter is right. I should stay out of things like this. I don't know why I always feel like I have to investigate," I said.

Anabel grabbed my arm. "Actually, you should investigate."

"Me?"

"Yes." She leaned toward me and whispered, "Chief Tyler is corrupt. There's no telling how he'll handle this investigation. If we want to get to the bottom of this, you need to take charge."

"Corrupt? Did Tiny tell you that?" I asked.

"Yes. A couple of years ago, he came home one night really upset," she said.

"Were his eyebrows twitching?" I asked.

Anabel looked perplexed. "Huh?"

"Never mind, go on," I said.

"Well, he had a few shots of whiskey, something he never does, then told me how Chief Tyler covered up a drug smuggling ring that was being run out of Destiny Key."

"Why didn't Tiny report it?" I asked.

"He did. It went all the way to the state attorney, but then the case was mysteriously dropped. This island takes care of its own. They have enough money to buy anyone." Anabel paced back and forth on the dock, clenching her fists. "Don't you want to see justice done? Don't you want to make sure an innocent person isn't accused of murder? Because that's what Chief Tyler will do—he'll try to pin this on whoever is the easiest scapegoat. He won't waste any time looking for clues, interviewing witnesses, gathering evidence—"

"Did you say interviewing witnesses? Do you think someone saw Gregor get killed?" I asked, interrupting Anabel's tirade.

"I don't know if there are any witnesses, but that's what a good investigator does—find out if there are. And you're a good investigator," she said.

"I am?"

"Of course. Look at how many murders you've solved in Coconut Cove already."

"I'm pretty sure your ex would beg to differ," I said. "He's taken credit for every one of them."

She smiled. "Well, that's true. But I do know that he thinks the help you provided aided in cracking the cases."

I was stunned. "He said that?"

"Well, not in so many words," she admitted.

"What exactly has he said?"

"Uh..." She grinned, then covered her mouth to stifle her laughter.

"That's what I thought." I looked at her hands. "Are you wearing your engagement ring again?"

Her face reddened. "Well, yes, but it's on my right hand, not my left."

"But it's still your engagement ring, right?" I asked.

"It's pretty, that's all." She held out her hand to admire it. "Seems a shame to let it sit in a jewelry box."

"I knew it," I said. "You two are getting back together."

She twisted the ring on her finger. "No, we're not. That ship has sailed."

"You've also been spending lots of time together lately," I pointed out.

"That's because we have joint custody of Frick and Frack. We're just friends."

"Would you even tell me if the two of you were seeing each other romantically, or would you keep it a secret like Victoria did?"

"Can we just drop the subject?" Anabel said. She pointed at the dinghy. "Looks like the seagulls are back."

While Mrs. Moto ran back and forth making a chirping sound, I reached down to jostle the side of the dinghy. "Get off there!"

After they flew away, the calico lay down on the dock and started washing herself.

"Strong work. You deserve a rest break," I told her, then sat on the edge of the dock. I pulled out Scooter's phone and took some pictures.

"See, you're already investigating," Anabel said.

"These are just photos," I said.

"It's more than that, admit it."

"Fine, I'm curious about who did this and why."

She clapped her hands together. "Great, you're in. I'll tell you what, I'll be your assistant. What's our first step?"

"Step number one is to find the murder weapon."

"That'll be tricky," Anabel said.

"No. I think it's going to be a cinch." While I had been

jostling the dinghy to scare off the birds, something rolled out from underneath the body. "See that there?" I asked. "I'm pretty sure that's the knife that killed Gregor."

CHAPTER 6
KILLER DOLPHINS

"What's going on down here?" a man's voice said.

Both Anabel and I startled. We had been so engrossed in looking at the knife next to Gregor's body that we hadn't noticed that anyone had joined us.

I looked up and saw Ben standing behind us, his hands jammed in the pockets of his tattered khaki shorts and his hair pulled back in its usual ponytail. He glanced at the dinghy and whistled. "Looks like you've got another one on your hands, Mollie. What does that make? Six bodies now?"

I ignored his question about my body count. "What are you doing here?"

"Olivia and Sawyer are curious about what's going on. They sent me down to get an update." Ben rocked back and forth on his heels. "I ran into Thomas in the hallway when he came back in the house. He seemed pretty out of sorts so I followed him into the kitchen. Then he told me that Gregor was dead, but wouldn't give me any details."

My stomach grumbled at the thought of food. My

adrenaline had worn off and I needed to replace it with some caffeine, carbs, and sugar. "Was he making breakfast?"

"He said something about Dutch pancakes and muffins before he shooed me out of the kitchen, saying that he needed to be alone," Ben said.

"Did you tell the girls what Thomas said about Gregor?"

"Yep," the young man said.

I cocked my head to one side. "And what was their reaction?"

"They asked what happened, and that's when I said I'd check it out," he said.

"Did they seem upset or shocked?" I asked.

Ben scratched his head. "Not really, now that you mention it. More curious than anything."

"That's kind of odd," Anabel said. "Wouldn't you be shocked if you heard someone had been murdered?"

The young man's eyes widened. "Murdered?" He looked more closely at the dinghy. "Is that blood and a stab wound?" After I nodded, he said, "Wow. We just assumed he had a heart attack."

"Good," I said. "We need to keep it that way. You can't tell Olivia and Sawyer what you've seen here."

"How are you going to keep it a secret?" Anabel asked me. "Thomas already knows he was murdered and so does Victoria. They both saw the body."

"True, but they don't know about that." I pointed at the knife. "If we want to figure out who did it, we need to keep details of the murder weapon strictly between us. The less we tell people, the better."

"I see," Ben said. "You're hoping the murderer will trip up and mention something about the knife."

"Exactly," I said. "Only the killer will know exactly what type of knife he was stabbed with." I looked at Ben. "Can you keep this a secret? Even from Sawyer?"

"Sure. I'd rather talk to her about other things, anyway."

He gave me a goofy smile. "I think she wants to go out with me."

"What makes you think that?" I asked.

"I suggested that she come out sailing with me sometime," he said.

"What did she say?" I asked.

"Nothing really," he said. "But she didn't say no, so I'm counting that as a win."

That's one of the things I loved about Ben. No matter how many times women turned him down, or, in Sawyer's case, avoided committing to a date, he still kept trying. Sawyer seemed like a nice girl. I hoped she ended up saying yes to going out with him. Provided she wasn't the murderer, of course.

Then I shook my head and pointed at the dinghy. "I'm not sure talking about your love life is appropriate given the circumstances."

"Did you speak with Victoria on your way over here?" Anabel asked. We all looked over at the grief-stricken woman who was still wading in the water. Her toes must have been like prunes by that point.

"I tried to, but she wasn't very talkative," Ben said. "Neither was Scooter."

"When did you see him?" I asked.

"When I was walking down here. He was heading back to the house. He said something about wanting a cup of cocoa." Ben tugged at his t-shirt. "I don't know how he can think about drinking a hot beverage. Man, is it ever sticky. And it's still early. It's going to be a humid one today."

"It's the chocolate. It helps him deal with what happened." I sighed. "What I wouldn't give for some chocolate now too."

"How can you be thinking about food at a time like this?" Anabel asked. "You need to stay focused on your job."

"Her job?" Ben asked.

"Yes, she's investigating the murder," Anabel said.

"Cool. Do you need help?" he said. "I could be your deputy and wear one of those badges like they do in the movies."

I smiled. "I don't think a badge will be necessary."

"Okay, boss. Whatever you say." He rubbed his hands together. "What should we do first?"

I furrowed my brow. "I'm not sure. The only investigations I've led officially were as an investigative reporter for FAROUT, and those had to do with alien abductions. This is a bit different." I turned to Anabel. "What does Tiny normally do in a case like this?"

She considered this for a moment before saying, "We should secure the crime scene."

"But we don't have any of that yellow police tape," I said.

"Why don't I go back to the house and see if Thomas has anything we can use?" Ben offered.

"Sounds good. And while you're at it, can you bring us back a couple of muffins?" I asked.

"Sure thing."

As he started to walk down the dock, I added, "Coffee would be great too." He gave me a thumbs up sign.

"Why would Gregor be out at the dock in the middle of the night?" Anabel asked.

"That's a good question." I tapped my finger on my lips. "Did the killer arrange to meet him here? Did he go out for a walk and then was surprised by the killer? Obviously, I don't think we can answer those questions yet, but we should try to narrow down the timeframe when the murder took place."

"Well, we all went to bed around eleven," Anabel said.

"And I found the body around six this morning."

"So it happened sometime between eleven pm and six am," she said.

I looked at the branches, coconuts, and palm fronds littering the beach. "Do you think he would have really come down here during the storm?"

"Good point," Anabel said. "I know the storm was still

raging at three-thirty. A branch fell on the roof over my room and it woke me up. I remember checking the time after I looked out the window to see what had happened."

"Did you see anyone on the dock or beach?"

"My room faces the rear of the house. I don't have a view in this direction. Honestly, with the rain coming down as hard as it was, I wouldn't have been able to make out anyone, anyway. And, like you said, it's unlikely anyone would have been outside then."

"I wonder if anyone else saw anything during the night?" I mused.

Anabel chewed on her lip. "Well, Victoria and Thomas' rooms face the beach, so one of them might have seen something. The one that Sawyer and Olivia are sharing is in the back, next to mine."

"I wish I had a notebook," I said. "We really need to write down a list of things to do, like ask Victoria and Thomas if they saw anything, either during the storm or after."

"And ask Victoria if she noticed Gregor leaving their room and, if so, at what time," Anabel added.

"Here you go, ladies," Ben said as he rejoined us. He handed us each a muffin, then pulled a bunch of scarves out of the tote bag slung over his shoulder. "Will these work? I figure we can tie the scarves together to use as a makeshift rope."

"Very creative," I said. "Where did you find those?"

"In an old trunk at the bottom of the stairs," he said, holding up a paisley scarf. "There's all sorts of cool things in there like a gladiator shield, wigs, and costumes."

"Thomas did say that the owner is in the theater," Anabel said. "Maybe they're from plays he's been in."

As Ben tied the scarves together, I wolfed down my muffin. Anabel ate hers at a daintier pace.

"How's that?" he asked, holding up his handiwork.

"Looks good," I said.

He pointed at the end of the dock by the beach. "I figured we could tie one end to the pole on that side of the dock and the other end on the opposite pole. That way no one will be able to walk up here and disturb the crime scene."

As I tucked my unruly hair behind my ears, I felt sweat dripping down my neck. "I'm kind of getting worried about the heat out here. The hot sun and dead bodies don't really go well together. Maybe we should drag the dinghy onto shore and find a tarp to put over it."

"No problem. I'll pull it down there," Ben said, tucking the scarves into one of his pockets. He untied the line securing the dinghy to the cleat, then started to walk it down the dock. After a few feet, he said, "Um, it's stuck, boss."

"Oh, that'll be the stern anchor," I said.

"Here, I'll get it," Anabel offered. She leaned down and pulled on the line attached to the back of the dinghy. After she had hoisted the anchor out of the water, she held it up. "What should I do with it?"

"Well, I don't think we should toss it in the dinghy," I said. "It will contaminate the crime scene. And I don't want to leave it here, because the dock is also part of the crime scene. Do you mind carrying it down to the beach?"

Anabel pointed at a shed near the house. "Why don't I tuck it inside there? That way no one will accidentally step on it and it will be out of the way."

While Ben walked the dinghy down the rest of the dock and Anabel stored the anchor, I watched Victoria. She was now sitting on the beach, her legs crossed in front of her, stroking Mrs. Moto. As aloof as cats could be at times, Mrs. Moto always seemed to know when someone needed to be comforted.

"Gosh, that was heavy," Ben said as he positioned the dinghy on the beach. "Guess that's what happens when you're dragging dead weight. Get it? Dead weight?"

"Hilarious," I said.

"Police sometimes make jokes like that," Anabel said. "Helps relieve the tension when they have to deal with horrific things."

"Do you think I should apply to the police academy?" Ben asked. "I think I might be a natural at this."

"You realize it's nothing like the movies, right?" I said. "Besides, I can't see you giving up sailing. It's in your blood."

"True." He pointed at the scarves hanging out of his shorts' pocket. "What should I do with these?"

I looked at the area around the dinghy. "There's really no way to cordon this area off. Maybe we should focus on collecting the evidence instead. We'll need some plastic bags."

"On it, boss." Ben raced back to the house, reappearing a few minutes later. He reached into the tote bag. "Okay, I have bags, a marker, and two more muffins."

I inhaled my muffin in less time than it took Anabel to peel the paper wrapper off the bottom of hers. Then I bent down and started to reach for the knife. "Oops. I don't want to get my fingerprints on this."

"You really don't," Anabel said in between bites. "Chief Tyler would decide you're his prime suspect based on the prints and arrest you without any further investigation. In addition to being corrupt, he's also lazy." She pulled an embroidered handkerchief out of her pocket and handed it to me. "Use this."

"That's adorable," I said. "Are those tiny unicorns?"

"Uh-huh. And next to them are elves," she said.

"This is gorgeous," I said, holding it up. "I don't want to ruin this picking up the knife."

"It's okay. It's for a good cause."

I gingerly grabbed the knife with the handkerchief. Ben held a bag open while I dropped the murder weapon inside. Then he handed me a pen.

"What do you think I should mark on it?" I asked.

"The date and time?" Ben suggested.

I scrawled those down, then added my initials and 'DD-001'.

Anabel stared at the bag. "What does 'DD-001' stand for?"

"It's our case number. 'DD' stands for 'dead in the dinghy' and this is evidence item number one."

"I think Tiny would be impressed," Anabel said.

Ben held out another bag. "What else do you have?"

"Only our stuff—the cooler, the gas tank, and the broken oar locks. Wait, what's that?" I pointed at a brown object lodged underneath the cooler. I used Anabel's handkerchief to pull out what looked like a matted clump of something unpleasant. Had Mrs. Moto hacked up a hairball in the dinghy when we weren't looking?

"Is that hair?" Ben asked.

"It could be." I set the handkerchief down on the beach, took a picture, then grabbed a small twig and pulled it apart. "I think you're right. It looks like long brown hair." I inserted it into a bag, marking it 'DD-002.'

Ben tugged at his brown ponytail self-consciously. "It's not mine."

"Strange how it's matted like that," I said, looking at the hair through the plastic.

"Almost like someone pulled a clump out of someone's head," Anabel said.

"During a struggle?" Ben asked.

She nodded. "Exactly."

"Well Gregor's hair is black so it isn't his." I looked at Anabel's fiery red hair piled on top of her head. "I think it's safe to rule you out."

"Ooh. Is this where you go through your list of suspects?" Ben asked.

"I guess," I said. "It had to have been someone here at the house."

"Someone could have come on foot," Ben said.

"I'm not sure about that," Anabel said. "Thomas said that the nearest house is pretty far away, and who in their right mind would have trekked through that storm to get here?"

"You're right," I said. "We should focus on who's here at Warlock Manor. Obviously, we're ruling out the three of us and Scooter. That leaves us with Sawyer—"

"She has blond hair," Ben said quickly.

"Right. And Olivia's hair is blue. Thomas has gray hair. That leaves us with..."

As my voice trailed off, the three of us turned and looked at Victoria sitting on the beach, her long brown hair cascading down her back.

* * *

"You think that's Victoria's hair?" Ben asked.

"Whose else could it be?" I replied. "I know this wasn't in the dinghy yesterday. Scooter cleaned it out before we left for the barbecue."

"It could have been blown in there during the storm," Anabel said.

Having learned the hard way that it was important not to jump to conclusions when conducting an investigation, I considered this carefully. Maybe Anabel was right, and the hair was unrelated to the murder. I bent down and examined the body more closely. "Do you see that?" I asked. "Gregor seems to have some strands of hair in his hand, and it looks like there are some caught in his signet ring. I'm not sure a storm can explain that."

"You're probably correct," Anabel said. "But it's so hard to believe that Victoria is a killer."

I gazed off into the distance. "I don't like the idea either, but remember what Gregor told your ex about her mental health. Maybe she went off the deep end."

"Should I put her under arrest?" Ben asked, eager to

undertake his self-appointed deputy duties.

"We're not in the arresting business," I said. "Our job is to present a case to the authorities and then let them take it from there. Do either of you see anything else we might have overlooked?"

While the three of us examined the dinghy, a dark four-wheel-drive vehicle pulled up in front of Warlock's Manor. A tall, scrawny man dressed in olive green cargo shorts and a light green short-sleeved shirt got out. He walked over to a garden shed where Anabel had stowed the stern anchor and opened the door.

"Who do you think that is?" Anabel asked.

"The gardener?" I suggested.

"Hey, that means the road is clear," Ben said. "The police should be here soon."

I had to admit that I was disappointed. Now that we had found two important clues—the knife and the clump of hair—and had a potential suspect, I was loath to give up the investigation. Not many police officers could solve a murder in a couple of hours like we had, I thought as I mentally patted myself on the back.

"Look, he's coming back out," Ben said. "What's that he's carrying?"

The man had a large brown sack in his arms. He opened up the rear door of his vehicle and deposited it in the back.

"Could it be potting soil or mulch?" I asked.

"Why would he be putting it in his car?" Anabel asked. "Shouldn't he be using it in the garden?"

We watched as the man repeated the process two more times.

"Something isn't right about this." I said. "I don't think those bags belong to him."

"Want me to arrest him?" Ben offered.

"I was thinking more along the lines of telling Thomas," I said.

"Why don't I do that?" Anabel offered.

As she walked away, she said over her shoulder, "Don't worry, Mollie. I'll get you another muffin."

Before she could reach the house, Thomas came out and greeted the scrawny man before pointing to where we were standing. The man nodded, clicked his car doors locked, then sauntered down the beach with Thomas at his side and Anabel trailing behind.

"This is Chief Tyler," Thomas said when they reached us.

"You're the chief of police?" Ben asked. "Shouldn't you be wearing a uniform?"

The chief stared down his long crooked nose at Ben. "And you are?" he asked in a voice that sent chills down my spine.

"Ben Moretti," he stammered.

"Wait here," Chief Tyler said.

He returned to his car, opened it, and reached into his glove box.

"Do you think he's getting a gun?" Ben whispered. "Maybe I shouldn't have said anything about what he was wearing."

"A gun would seem like a bit of an extreme reaction," I said. "Shush, he's coming back."

The chief had a small notebook in one hand and a pen in the other. He opened up the notebook, then stepped so close to Ben that I was sure they could see the pores on each other's faces. "Spell Moretti."

After Ben spelled his last name, he turned to Anabel. "Name?"

"Anabel Dalton."

He scowled. "Dalton? Any relation to Chief Dalton in Coconut Cove?"

"Yes, he's my husband. I mean my ex-husband."

He looked Anabel up and down. "Interesting," he said, writing something down in his notebook.

He didn't even bother to ask me what my name was. He simply stared at me until I spluttered, "Mollie McGhie." When he didn't add my name to his notebook, I didn't know whether to be offended or relieved.

"What's that?" he asked, pointing at Ben's shorts pocket.

"Scarves," Ben said nervously. "It's not a crime to have scarves, is it?"

"Hand them over." The young man shook as he gave the chief the scarves. Chief Tyler inspected the knots Ben had made, then wadded up the improvised rope and stuffed it in his own pocket.

"Do you think he's going to stash that in the back of his car like those bags?" Ben whispered in my ear.

The chief stared at Ben for a few uncomfortable moments, turned to a new page in his notebook, and jotted something down.

"Maybe I should go back to the house and see how everyone is doing," Ben suggested.

"No," was the monosyllabic reply from the chief.

"Did you want to examine the body?" Thomas asked.

The chief took one step toward the dinghy, looked at Gregor for a few seconds, then said, "Accidental death."

"Accidental? Did you see that gaping wound in his chest?" I said. "This is murder."

The chief fiddled with his notebook as though he was going to write something down before snapping it shut and tucking it in his shirt pocket.

"He drowned," Chief Tyler said with finality.

"How would someone who drowned end up in a dinghy stabbed to death?" I argued.

He shrugged. "Dolphins?"

"You're saying a dolphin swam into the inlet, through the mangroves, into this cove, then somehow stabbed Gregor before hoisting his body into the dinghy?"

"This is Destiny Key," the chief said, as though that explained it.

"I told you this island is unusual," Thomas said quietly.

I shook my head. "Killer dolphins kind of go above and beyond unusual."

The chief walked back to his car and opened the passenger door.

"See I told you, he's stealing the scarves," Ben said.

"No, he's not," Anabel said. "Wait a minute, I guess he is." We watched as he pulled the scarves out of his pocket slowly, like a magician does, before tossing them on the seat.

"Now I really want to know what's in those bags," Ben said.

"What bags?" Thomas asked.

"He took three bags out of the garden shed and put them in his car," Ben said. "You should ask him about it."

"Me? No," Thomas said. "I just want to get this over with."

"Get this over with?" I asked. "You mean you're happy that he thinks it was an accidental death?"

"Maybe it was," Thomas said. "That might be best."

"What? You want the killer to get away with it?" I asked.

"I'm not saying that," he said, crossing his arms across his chest. "But I think we can all agree that Gregor got what he deserved. Maybe we should just consider it justice served."

Anabel chewed on her lip, then slowly nodded.

"You think he's right, don't you?" I asked her.

Before she could respond, the chief returned. "Everyone needs to leave the island."

"We're leaving on the ferry on Tuesday morning," Thomas said.

"No," Chief Tyler said.

"Yes, we are," Thomas replied.

"No," he repeated. "You'll leave now."

"Why would we do that?" Thomas asked.

The chief looked back at the dinghy before responding. "Because I said so."

"Even if we wanted to leave," Anabel said, "there's no way off the island until Tuesday. The ferries don't run on the weekends or Mondays."

He shrugged. "I don't care how you get off the island. Just do it. There are plenty of boats anchored nearby. Get a ride on one of them. This is private property. If you're still here when I return, I'll consider you to be trespassers. We don't take kindly to trespassers on Destiny Key." Then he abruptly turned and walked back to his vehicle.

"Did you forget something?" I shouted.

He spun around, marched back to me, and snatched the evidence bags out of my hands.

As he clicked open his car doors, I shouted, "I meant the body!"

* * *

"Now what are we supposed to do?" Anabel asked. "We're stuck on this island until Tuesday with that insane chief of police who is insisting we leave immediately."

"I'm not leaving," Thomas said. "Michael gave me permission to use his house."

"Didn't you say that he and Chief Tyler are cousins?" Anabel asked.

Thomas nodded.

"Maybe you can talk to Michael and tell him what's going on and he can straighten things out with the chief."

"Even if I had cell phone service, which I still don't, I doubt if I could track him down," Thomas said. "He's off doing a play somewhere in Tuscany."

"We need to tell someone about what's going on," I said. "Maybe we can get a hold of Tiny on the VHF."

"They won't be able to hear us back in Coconut Cove," Thomas said. "The range is limited."

"Guys, remember, Chief Tyler drove in here, which means the road is clear," Ben said. "We can drive down to the public beach and get Penny to meet us there. She can take us back to the regatta boats where there's cell phone coverage and we can call Chief Dalton."

"Smart thinking," I said. Ben beamed at the compliment.

"We should get a move on before he gets back," Anabel said. "I can go there with Ben."

"Take Michael's golf cart to the trailhead that leads to the public beach. You'll see a sign marking the entrance," Thomas said. "While you're doing that, I'll hail *Pretty in Pink* and *Marjorie Jane* on the VHF and let them know what's going on."

"Hey, when you go back to the house, it might be better if you didn't tell anyone that Gregor has been murdered or about the evidence," I said.

"What evidence?" he asked.

"The bags Chief Tyler grabbed from me," I said.

"Oh, I must have missed that," he said. "What was in them?"

I breathed a sigh of relief. That meant that Thomas didn't know about the knife or the clump of hair. I improvised. "Nothing important. Just some sand and seashells we found next to Gregor."

"What are we going to do about him?" Ben asked, pointing at the dinghy.

"I'll stay with the body," I offered.

After everyone left, I paced on the beach while keeping the dinghy in my sights. There was no way that this was an accidental death. Or a murder by a dolphin. I wasn't sure which idea was more preposterous. Gregor was clearly murdered with a knife by a human. From what Anabel had said, the chief would probably bury the evidence, so I was glad that I had taken photos. But pictures might not be enough to prove what had really happened to the higher-up authorities, whoever that might be. What I needed was something tangible.

I looked inside the dinghy again, hoping to find something else that would confirm that the killer was Victoria. Sweat poured off me while I examined the crime scene. The body really should be covered, I thought. Not just out of respect, but also because of the hot sun beating down on it. I decided to poke in the shed and see if I could find something I could use. When I opened the door, a spider ran out. Where was Mrs. Moto when you needed her? In addition to being a good seagull-chaser-offer, she was also an expert at insect management.

I spotted a tarp on one of the shelving units at the back of the shed. As I reached up to pull it down, another spider ran down my arm. I shrieked and jumped back, tripped on a ladder and then fell onto the ground. As I sat up, I noticed a crumpled up piece of paper wedged by the door. I smoothed it out, keeping a careful eye out for other spiders, and examined it.

The paper looked like it was a note that had been ripped in half. I appeared to be holding the top portion. It was written in some sort of strange alphabet with 'Es' which had three dots on top of them and backwards 'Rs'. Was it some sort of code? As I tried to decipher it, I heard a vehicle pull up. I peeked out of the shed and saw a white van. Chief Tyler pulled up behind them in his four-wheel drive.

When two men got out of the van, I tucked myself behind the shed door so they wouldn't see me. Both of them were large and intimidating. Clearly, they spent a lot of time drinking protein drinks and lifting weights. The chief motioned to the dinghy then stepped back and watched as they carried Gregor's body to the van and placed him inside.

As they drove off, I wondered where they were taking Gregor. Was Destiny Key large enough to have its own coroner, or did Chief Tyler have other plans for the body?

CHAPTER 7
THE UNICORNS OF THE SEA

One of the goons slammed the rear van doors shut, while the other spoke with Chief Tyler. As the chief's henchmen drove away, he walked toward the shed. The thought of encountering the chief on my own made me nervous, so I looked around to see if there was a place I could hide that wasn't already inhabited by spiders. While I was deciding between a spot behind one of the shelving units or tucking myself under the tarp, I heard Thomas beckon the chief over to the house.

While the chief and Thomas spoke, I slipped out of the shed and crept down to the beach, then casually sauntered along the water as though I had been strolling there all along. I tried to hear what the two men were saying, but the seagulls were making too much noise squabbling with each other over who was in charge of that particular section of the beach. The birds scattered when Ben pulled up in the golf cart and sounded the horn.

I hurried over to get an update. "Where's Anabel?"

"She's still on the public beach. She managed to get cell phone reception, so she's giving Chief Dalton an update."

"And what about Penny?" I asked.

"She's gone back to round up another dinghy to ferry people to the boats," he said. "It's a shame yours is still out of commission."

"If only that was just because the engine wasn't working," I said. "It puts a whole new spin on things when someone has died in your dinghy."

Ben smiled wryly. "Anyway, I told her I'd collect everyone, and we'd meet her back there in about an hour."

"All right. Do you mind telling Victoria about the plan? She's still sitting on the beach over there."

He nodded.

"And I'll let Thomas and the girls know."

After I explained the arrangements to Thomas, Chief Tyler looked at his watch. "You have exactly sixty minutes from now to vacate the island."

Thomas folded his arms across his chest. "Like I said, I'm not leaving. Your cousin said I can stay here."

"Do you have proof?" the chief asked.

"As a matter of fact, I do," Thomas said. "Wait here and I'll get it."

The chief and I played the staring game while we waited. I have to say, he was a highly skilled opponent. His steely gaze never wavered, not even for a second. But I was determined to win, so I casually said, "What was in those bags you took from the shed and put in your vehicle?"

He blinked rapidly, then spun around to look at the shed before pulling his keychain from his pocket and clicking it to make sure that his four-wheel drive was locked.

Before I could follow up, Thomas approached us waving a piece of paper in his hands. "Here's the email from Michael." He thrust it at the chief. "See, it says that he gives me permission to stay here. It also goes on to say how much he appreciates me watching over the place so that nothing goes missing."

"Hmm. Sounds like Michael might have been worried that something would get stolen from Warlock's Manor," I said. "I wonder what that could be?"

Chief Tyler pursed his lips. "Fine, you can stay until Tuesday. But then you better be on that ferry or else."

I wasn't sure if it was the email that changed the chief's mind or the fact that he didn't want to discuss what exactly he had taken from the shed. Regardless of the reason, he left in a hurry.

Ben made a couple of trips, chauffeuring Sawyer, Olivia, Victoria, and their luggage to the public beach. Afterward, he returned with Anabel so that she could collect her belongings.

"Penny asked about Gregor's death," Ben said as he carried Anabel's suitcase to the golf cart. "I told him that Chief Tyler said it was an accidental death. I figured it would be better to go with that story while we're investigating the murder."

"That was a good idea," I said. "The killer might slip up if they think they got away with it."

He grinned. "I'm getting the hang of this detective work."

"Was Victoria there when you said that?"

He nodded.

"She saw Gregor's body. Surely, she doesn't think it was an accident."

"She seemed to go along with it," he said. "To tell you the truth, she seemed pretty hazy about seeing Gregor. She said the shock was overwhelming and she can't remember much."

I looked around at our group. The only people who knew for certain that a murder had taken place were Anabel, Ben, Scooter, and me. And the murderer, of course. Everyone else thought it had been an accident, oblivious to the fact that Victoria, Sawyer, Olivia, or Thomas could be a killer.

On the way to the beach we had talked about who could have done it. "Victoria seems like the most likely candidate given the hair we found," I said.

At first, Anabel defended her friend, then she said, "Even if she did do it, it must have been out of some sort of jealous rage that was specifically directed at Gregor. It's not like she's going to attack anyone else. Not that I think she killed him," she added hastily.

"What do you think, Scooter?" I asked.

"I don't want to think about it," he said.

"Well, that's one approach," I said. "We can pretend it didn't happen."

He smiled. "I'm pretty sure you won't be able to do that. You'll be thinking about it non-stop until you figure out who did it. But the rest of us can pretend."

The golf cart swerved as Ben avoided a large branch. "I agree with Anabel. If Victoria did it, she's not going to go after anyone else. I actually feel bad for her. Every time I look at her, she's crying her eyes out."

"We can't rule Thomas out," Anabel said. "He hated Gregor."

"What about the girls?" I asked.

"What reason would they have to want Gregor dead?" Ben asked.

"I'm not sure, but that's what makes being a detective so interesting," I said. "You uncover all sorts of secrets."

"Hopefully, the only secret Sawyer has is that she has a crush on me," Ben said.

When we got to the beach, Penny was there along with a couple of other people who had offered their dinghies up as a sort of taxi service. After talking about who should go where, I said, "We can take Anabel on *Marjorie Jane*."

Victoria was sitting on a piece of driftwood by herself, dabbing at her eyes.

"Would you be able to take Victoria as well?" Anabel asked me. "She's going through a lot and I feel like I should be with her. I'm the person she's closest to here."

"It'll be a tight squeeze," I said. "We already have Melvin and Ben on board."

"I can sleep on deck," Ben offered. "That'll leave room for Victoria and Anabel to sleep in the main cabin."

"Are you sure?" I asked.

"Yeah, it'll be fun," Ben said. "Like being back in Sea Scouts."

"Okay," I said. "We'll take the two of them. Now what about Sawyer and Olivia?"

"Some of the people I have crewing on my boat are going to move to other boats, so I have room for Sawyer and Olivia on *Pretty in Pink*," Penny offered. The arrangements settled, we all headed off to our respective boats. As I looked at Sawyer and Olivia sitting in Penny's dinghy, I hoped that she hadn't ended up hosting a killer on board her boat.

* * *

The next morning, I was the second-to-last person up. I stretched my arms over my head as I looked at the other regatta boats in the anchorage. Although Chief Tyler had ordered us off the island, he hadn't had the authority to tell us to leave the surrounding waters, so we had all stayed put.

Everyone except Ben was gathered in the cockpit, sipping coffee. He was stretched out on the deck by the bow, snoring gently, oblivious to the others chatting about the dolphins frolicking in the bay. Melvin and Anabel were discussing the types of dolphins found in Florida and the Bahamas. She was partial to the Atlantic spotted variety; he preferred the more common bottlenose ones. Victoria chimed in to say that she thought dolphins were overrated and that manatees were far more interesting.

"How did you sleep, my little stegosaurus?" Scooter asked as he poured a cup of coffee for me.

"Fine," I said, which was a lie. I had spent most of the night awake, tossing and turning while I thought about Gregor's murder.

"Anyone hungry?" Scooter asked. "Why don't I fix us some grub?"

"I'll help," Melvin said.

While the guys fixed breakfast, I casually asked Victoria about her relationship with Gregor. Her face lit up as she talked about how their romance started. "I was at a reception at an art gallery when I saw this distinguished man standing by the bar. He was impeccably dressed in a black suit. I could tell right away that it had been custom tailored for him."

"So he was rich?" I asked.

"Yes," she said. "But he was generous with his money. He took me on a trip to Saint Petersburg with him. We stayed at the finest hotels, ate at the most exquisite restaurants, and went for romantic walks along the Neva River in the moonlight." She clapped her hands together with excitement. "The best part of the trip was when we visited the Winter Palace. The art was incredible."

"The Winter Palace?" I asked. "I don't think I've been there. We'll have to check it out next time we visit. Scooter wants to see a Cleveland Indians-Tampa Bay Rays game during the fall."

Anabel leaned over. "She means the Saint Petersburg in Russia, not the one in Florida."

"Oh," I said, slightly embarrassed. "Never been to that one. Guess I'm not very well traveled."

"You have to go," Victoria said. "If nothing else, go for the art at the Hermitage. To be able to see original Gauguins in person should be on everyone's bucket list."

I had no idea what Gauguins were, and I didn't want to show my ignorance by asking, so I murmured something about adding it to my list.

"What a treat that must have been," Anabel said. "That was a couple of months ago, right? I didn't realize that trip had been with Gregor."

Victoria took a sip of coffee. "He didn't want anyone to know."

"Didn't that bother you?" I asked. "When I fell in love with Scooter, I was shouting it from the rooftop."

Victoria looked irritated. "You were probably young when you met Scooter. When you're more mature, you don't need to brag about that sort of thing."

"I wasn't bragging," I said. "I was just happy."

"Breakfast is ready," Scooter said as he passed up platters of bacon, scrambled eggs, and toast.

Ben sat up and rubbed his eyes. "Did you say breakfast?"

"Yep, come and get it," Scooter said.

Ben walked over to the cockpit, snagged a piece of bacon and wolfed it down. "Can you save me some eggs? I want to take a quick dip first." He pulled off his t-shirt, then jumped off the boat, hugging his knees to his chest and cannonballed into the water, splashing the rest of us in the process. "Whoo-hoo!" he said after he surfaced. "You guys should join me. The water feels great."

Mrs. Moto bounded off my lap, raced to the side of the boat and meowed as though to say, "Wait for me." Then she dived in and paddled after Ben.

"We have to do something about that cat," Scooter said.

* * *

"Are you missing a crew member?" Ned asked, as he pulled Penny's dinghy, *Pinkie*, alongside *Marjorie Jane*. He cut the motor while grabbing the side of our boat to keep from drifting away.

"Thank you for rescuing her," Scooter said.

I looked at Nancy who was sitting at the front, scowling and holding a wet cat on her lap. "I'm surprised to see you cuddling her."

"This isn't cuddling," she snapped. "Every time Ned scooped her out of the water, she jumped right back in. I'm only holding her so she doesn't escape again."

"Are you sure she jumped in or did you push her in?" I joked.

"I may not like her, but I wouldn't try to drown her," Nancy said with a sniff. "This creature seems to want to be in the water."

"It's bizarre how she's taking a sudden liking to swimming," I said.

"I'm not surprised," Ned said. "Japanese bobtails are attracted to the water."

"Maybe that's why she loves Frisky Feline Ocean's Delight so much," Scooter said.

Mrs. Moto squirmed in Nancy's arms. "Take this mangy beast already," she said to me.

I lifted the soggy cat onto the deck. "No more swimming, okay?" I said. "If you promise to stay on board, you can have some bacon." The calico made an ambiguous chirping sound. "Is that a yes?" I asked.

"Hand her to me," Victoria offered. "I'll dry her off and make sure she stays put."

"Humph. Look what that creature did," Nancy said. Her shorts were covered with paw prints and some strands of seaweed.

"Sorry," I said. "Can I get you a towel? Or some bacon?"

"No, we can't stay. We're just making the rounds to see what everyone wants to do," Ned said. "After what happened yesterday, we ended up canceling the race that was planned. So maybe it might be best to cancel the rest of the regatta as well."

"That's a good point. Gregor's death was a big shock." I looked at Anabel and Victoria. "What would you ladies like to do? Do you want to head back to Coconut Cove today?"

Anabel held up her sketchbook. "I'm happy for the regatta

to continue. Staying on a sailboat is wonderful inspiration. I have all sorts of ideas for a new series of paintings featuring narwhals."

"What are narwhals?" Scooter asked.

"They're the unicorns of the sea," Anabel said.

"Unicorns aren't real, dear," Nancy said.

"Of course they are," Anabel said sharply.

The older woman shook her head. "No wonder you and Mollie are such good friends. You believe in unicorns and she believes in little green men. You girls have such overactive imaginations."

Anabel muttered something under her breath, then began furiously drawing with a charcoal pencil on her sketchpad.

"What about you, Victoria?" Scooter asked gently. "You and Gregor were engaged. We'd be happy to make our way back to Coconut Cove today."

"If you don't mind, I'd rather stay here for another day." She fed Mrs. Moto a piece of bacon, then continued. "The regatta will help take my mind off what happened. Plus it helps to be around other people."

"Well, as long as you're sure," he said.

She nodded.

"Okay, the crew of *Marjorie Jane* is up for it," Scooter said.

"What about Sawyer and Olivia?" I asked. "How are they holding up?"

"They're both upset, naturally," Nancy said. "But neither of them were close with Gregor. Olivia told us that she met him for the first time on Friday night when he turned up at Warlock's Manor. And Sawyer said he was only an acquaintance, someone she ran into occasionally at local art events."

"The girls are excited to race in the regatta," Ned said.

"And with someone with Olivia's level of sailing experience on board, there's no way *Pretty in Pink* can lose," Nancy said.

"It hardly seems fair that your crew gets Olivia," I said. "I still can't believe that you asked the folks who were already on *Pretty in Pink* to move to other boats so you could host Olivia and Sawyer. If we're going to handicap boats in the regatta races so they're on a level playing field, shouldn't we also handicap you guys because you have an unfair advantage in terms of the level of sailing expertise you have on board?"

"Life isn't fair, dear." She tapped Ned on the shoulder. "Ready to go? We have one last boat to check in with—the *Mistletoe*."

"Is that the catamaran?" I asked. "Such a cute boat name."

"You should see how they decorate it for Christmas," Ned said.

"It will be Christmas soon if we sit around here all day yapping," Nancy said. "Let's get a move on."

As Ned pointed their dinghy toward the catamaran, Victoria said, "She lied."

I turned to look at her. "Who lied?"

"Sawyer." Her jaw tightened. "She and Gregor weren't acquaintances. They were lovers."

* * *

Victoria clammed up after her pronouncement that Sawyer had lied about her relationship with Gregor, saying that it was too upsetting to talk about. Breakfast had gotten cold while we spoke with Ned and Nancy, but we all still dug in. There's something about being on the water that gives you an appetite. Or at least that was the excuse I gave for having a second helping.

After we ate, Ben and Mrs. Moto lay down on the deck at the front of the boat and napped, tuckered out by their morning swim. The guys went down below to look at charts and strategize for the day's race, while Anabel, Victoria and I had some more coffee.

I was surprised when Victoria started talking about

Sawyer. Maybe she felt more comfortable now that it was just us girls.

"She's a second-rate artist," she said bitterly. "She used Gregor for his connections in the art world."

"When did they break up?" I asked.

"At the reception I was telling you about," she said proudly. "He said that when he met me, he couldn't imagine being with anyone else. He told her it was over that night."

"Did she blame you for what happened?"

"No, she never knew. That's one of the reasons why he said he wanted to keep our relationship secret. Sawyer was upset. He didn't want her to take it out on me."

While she twirled the bracelet on her wrist, I wondered if it had been Sawyer who had destroyed Victoria's paintings as retribution.

After taking another sip of coffee, Victoria continued. "Gregor was driving her home that night. They stopped at the park and walked down to the waterfront. When he ended things, she grabbed his cane and threw it in the water, then stormed off."

"She just left him like that?" Anabel asked. "He couldn't walk very well without a cane, could he?"

"No," Victoria said. "He had to hobble back to the car. Fortunately, he had a spare cane at home."

"That carved one he had last night?" I asked.

"The one from Tahiti? No, he got that one later. His spare one was one of those metal ones."

"I'd love to go to Tahiti one day," Anabel said. Her phone buzzed. "I better get that. It's Tiny."

While she sat at the stern of the boat to speak with her ex, Victoria drank the rest of her coffee then went down below for a refill. I leaned back against the cushions. Mrs. Moto padded over and crawled into my lap. While I stroked her, I thought about Gregor's cane. It was almost like a piece of artwork in its own right with its intricate carvings and mother-of-pearl handle.

"Oh, my gosh," I said to Mrs. Moto. "The knife. The cane. They're connected. Can you believe it?" The calico yawned in response, rolled over on her back, and demanded belly rubs. I petted her with one hand and did a search on my phone with the other.

"What are you looking at?" Anabel asked as she sat next to me.

"Look at this," I said, holding up my cell.

"It's a cane," she said.

"Not just any cane," I said, swiping my phone. "Look at this picture. When you pull the handle out, there's a knife. Just like the one we found next to Gregor."

"So you think someone stabbed him with his own cane?"

"Uh-huh. And that person would have had to know there was a knife inside."

"Not necessarily," Anabel said. "Gregor could have pulled it out for self-defense and then the killer grabbed it from him."

"I don't think so. Remember how slippery the dock was? You saw Gregor. He couldn't stand on his own without his cane. There's no way he could have lifted it up and pulled the knife out without losing his balance. No, I think the killer took the cane from him, knowing there was a knife inside. Gregor probably grabbed one of the pilings for support. The killer stabbed him, then he either fell into the dinghy or he was pushed into it."

"So the murderer had to have known about the cane," Anabel said.

"Correct. It all points back to Victoria. She was seeing him when he got his new cane from Tahiti," I sad. "He probably showed it to her. She had to have known there was a hidden knife."

"Well, it doesn't really matter, in any event," Anabel said. "Tiny said that Chief Tyler has everyone convinced that it was an accidental death. There isn't going to be a formal investigation."

"But what about the evidence—the knife and the hair?"

"He denies there being any evidence," Anabel said.

"But we were there. We saw it. We bagged it."

"Do you really think anyone is going to believe us?" she asked. "They'll paint Ben as some sort of unreliable surfer dude. They'll say I'm making it up to get back at Chief Tyler on behalf of Tiny. And you..."

"What about me?" I asked.

"They'll bring up your involvement with FAROUT and how you believe in UFOs and alien abduction to discredit you. You'll end up a laughingstock."

"But we have photos," I said.

"Scooter is starting a YouTube channel, right? They'll say he knows all about editing videos and photos and that he doctored them. That they're fake."

I ran my fingers through my hair. "What are we going to do?"

"I'm not sure," she said. "Let's talk with Tiny when we get back to Coconut Cove tomorrow and come up with a game plan."

CHAPTER 8
THE GHOST OF COCONUT CARL

After the race that afternoon—and the less said about that the better, as we came in third place—everyone headed to the beach for the Fourth of July festivities. At first, there had been some debate as to whether we should skip the picnic and volleyball game, given Chief Tyler's threats about what he would do to trespassers on Destiny Key, but Nancy was adamant that the beach was public property and that we had every right to be there. In the end, everyone came around to her way of thinking.

While the rest of the *Marjorie Jane's* crew went ahead, I stayed behind to finish cooking my contribution to the potluck. My mother had sent me a cookbook specifically designed for cooking aboard a boat. She hadn't been hugely supportive of us moving aboard a sailboat, so I was surprised by the gift. But maybe it was her way of saying that she'd come around to the idea.

The dish I was making utilized canned ingredients, something sailors relied on when making long passages. As I looked at the recipe, I wondered what kind of food Olivia had eaten when she did her circumnavigation. After my chicken enchiladas came out of the oven, Ned and Nancy picked me up in *Pinkie* and we headed to shore.

"Thanks for the ride," I said, as Ned helped me out of the dinghy.

"No problem," he said. "It's hard to be carless when you're on a boat."

"Carless?" I asked.

"Boaters think of their dinghies like cars," he said. "It's how you get around. You need a reliable dinghy to get to shore, go shopping, head to snorkeling spots, or just to visit other boats."

"That makes sense," I said. "We really need our dinghy back."

"Why would you want it back?" Nancy asked. "Someone died in it."

I grimaced. "True. But it would cost a fortune to replace it. I'm not sure that our insurance company will allow us to make a claim on it due to murder."

"Murder," Ned said. "I thought it was an accident."

"Um…" I mumbled.

"Speak up, dear," Nancy said.

"It wasn't exactly an accident," I blurted out. "Someone killed him, but Chief Tyler is trying to cover it up."

"Someone?" Ned asked.

"My money's on Victoria," I said.

After I explained about the knife and hair that we had found, and that I thought Victoria had killed Gregor in a moment of jealous rage, Nancy surprised me by saying that she thought I should drop the investigation.

"Normally, I'm one for following the rules," she said. "But in this case, maybe it's best to leave things alone."

"But Chief Tyler is trying to cover it up," I said. "We can't let him get away with that. It's just like Roswell, all over again."

Ned gave me a blank look.

"You know, the government cover-up in the 1940s of an alien landing in New Mexico."

"Oh, I think I saw a movie about that once," Ned said.

"This is nothing like Roswell," Nancy said. "Flying saucers aren't responsible."

"Well, it's a bit like it," Ned said. Nancy shot him a look and he hastened to add, "No, there aren't any UFOs or alien life involved, but you know what they say about the ghost of Coconut Carl."

"Coconut Carl? The pirate?" I asked with surprise. The man they were referring to had been known in these parts for his love of plunder, booze, and women. There was a wooden statue of him at the Tipsy Pirate bar, which tourists flocked to see. They would rub his belly three times for good luck while drinking shots of rum. I had been known to do the same thing from time to time when I needed help with a case.

"The very same one," Ned said. "Legend has it that during a storm dolphins guided his cutter to safety to the cove in front of Warlock's Manor."

"But the inlet is shallow. How could he have sailed into the cove on a sailboat?"

"No one knows. That's part of what makes it so mysterious," Ned said. "But here's the interesting part. Once he was safely anchored, one of the dolphins turned into a beautiful woman and lured him to shore. While she plied him with drink, the other dolphins crept onto his boat—"

"How do dolphins creep onto anything?" I asked. "They don't have legs."

Nancy snorted. "Finally, you've said something logical."

Ned held up his hands. "I'm just telling you how the story goes. Anyway, the dolphins took all the gold from his boat and buried it somewhere on Destiny Key."

"What happened once Coconut Carl discovered his gold

was missing?" I asked.

"He never did find out about it...at least not while he was alive. As he was going back to his boat, a coconut fell off a tree and knocked him on his head. He died instantly. They say his ghost still haunts the island in search of his loot."

"There's no such thing as ghosts," I said.

Nancy nodded approvingly. "See, even Mollie doesn't believe that nonsense."

"How do you explain the freak storm yesterday then?" Ned asked. "That's the kind of mysterious thing that always happens on this island."

"I'm sure there's a perfectly reasonable explanation for the storm yesterday," she said. "Anyway, what's happening here doesn't have anything to do with ghosts, dolphins, or aliens. It has to do with that despicable man—Chief Tyler."

I furrowed my brow. "Anabel told me how he covered up drug smuggling, but why do I have a feeling there's more to it than that?"

Ned and Nancy exchanged glances, then he said, "The less you know, the better."

"It's safer if you drop the whole thing," Nancy said. "Let's just forget you ever said anything about a murder. Now, let's get this food over to the potluck. Grab that cooler, Ned."

As they bustled off, a chill ran down my spine. Maybe it wasn't such a good idea to have our picnic on Destiny Key. After what Ned and Nancy had said—or hadn't said—I was more afraid of the chief of police than I was of the fact that there was a murderer in our midst.

* * *

After depositing my dish with everyone else's, I walked over to where Olivia and Sawyer were sitting. Sawyer was leaning against a palm tree, sketching the boats at anchor. Olivia was running along the beach, waving a palm frond back and forth for Mrs. Moto to chase. "Do you mind if I join you?" I asked. "I brought some dinner over for the admiral."

As I set a plate of Frisky Feline Ocean's Delight down, Sawyer held up her sketchpad. "Do you like it?"

I was amazed at how she had captured *Marjorie Jane's* likeness, yet somehow made her look like she'd had a makeover. Maybe that's what she would look like once we finished fixing her up. "You're a wonderful artist," I said after looking at the drawings she had made of the other boats.

"Thanks," she said. "I'm thinking of turning them into note cards and selling them at the Sailor Corner Cafe."

"That's a great idea," I said. "Tourists will snap them up."

"That's what I figured," she said. "They like walking around the marina looking at the boats. The cards would be nice souvenirs."

"You should talk with Nancy about selling them at the marina office as well," I suggested.

"Good thought," she said. "You know, Thomas was the one who gave me the idea about the cards. I wonder how he's doing. Do you think we should walk up to Warlock's Manor and check on him?"

"I don't think that's a smart idea," I said. "We're kind of pushing our luck just being here on the beach."

"I suppose you're right." She pulled a box of oil pastels out of her backpack and started coloring in the sketch she had made of Marjorie Jane. "I'll give him a call later."

"Are you a self-taught artist?" I asked.

"No, I went to art school in New York City. That's how Olivia and I met. We were roommates."

"Was that where you met Gregor?" I asked. "He ran a school there."

"There are a lot of art schools in the city," she said.

"But you did know him, didn't you?" I asked.

"He's very famous in art circles. Everyone knows him." She looked at the uneaten plate of cat food. "Ben told me that

Mrs. Moto practically inhales wet food the minute you put it down. How come she hasn't had any of this?"

"That is a good question. She's either having too much fun playing with Olivia or she ate too much bacon this morning." I held up the plate and said, "Here kitty-kitty. Dinner time!"

Mrs. Moto looked up from the palm frond she was chewing, then bounded across the beach, kicking sand up behind her.

"See, she's inhaling it," I said to Sawyer as we watched the cat crouch over the plate.

Olivia plopped down next to me. "What have you guys been talking about?"

"We were talking about Gregor," I said.

"No, we were actually talking about Ben," Sawyer quickly said. "He loves Mrs. Moto. He'd love to have his own cat. Maybe I should get him a kitten. What do you think?"

"I'm not sure he'd be up for cleaning the litter box," I said. "Doing his own laundry on a regular basis is a challenge."

"I'd think twice about giving him a gift," Olivia said. "He might think you like him."

"I do like him," Sawyer said.

"You do?" I asked. "That's so great to hear. He's such a sweet guy."

"Oh, I don't like him like that. He's like a brother to me," Sawyer clarified. "I told him as much on Friday night."

"Not exactly what a guy wants to hear," Olivia said with a laugh. "He's too young for you, anyway."

"I thought the two of you went to high school together," I said. "That would make you the same age."

"She likes older men," Olivia said in a teasing voice.

"Scooter is older than me," I said.

"Is he really?" Olivia asked. "I wouldn't have guessed that."

I wasn't sure whether to be offended or not. "Yes, I'm younger."

"You can't be that much younger than him though," Olivia

said. "Sawyer likes guys who are way older."

Sawyer pulled a switchblade out of her bag, flipped it open then started sharpening one of her charcoal pencils.

"Wouldn't it be easier to use a pencil sharpener?" I asked.

"I like doing it this way. Reminds me of my father," Sawyer said.

"Ben said that you go hunting with him," I said.

"Used to. He passed away last year," she said.

"I'm sorry," I said.

"He had been really sick." She snapped her knife shut, then wistfully rubbed the intricately carved handle.

"That's beautiful," I said.

"Thanks. My dad carved it for me," she said. "Gave it to me for my twenty-first birthday."

"He was a very talented man," I said.

She nodded. "He made knives like these and sold them at fairs around the state. I would go with him and help. It was a lot of fun. We would do these knife-throwing demonstrations. It would really draw a crowd."

"You must miss him," I said.

Sawyer took a deep breath, then let it out slowly. "I do," she said, wiping away a tear.

Olivia motioned with her head to indicate I should give them a moment. As I walked away, I glanced over my shoulder at the two girls. I felt terrible that I had dredged up such awful memories. Death lingered on this island—not only the murder of Gregor, but also the memories of the death of Sawyer's father.

* * *

After everyone had eaten their fill, beach volleyball bragging rights had been established, and everyone danced to Penny's Fourth of July play list while waving sparklers, folks returned to their boats. A few of us had stayed behind, waiting for a dinghy to ferry us back. Ned and Scooter were making sure that the bonfire was completely out, Nancy was packing up a cooler, and Anabel and I were walking along the shore shell combing.

As I was picking up a piece of sea glass, I heard a voice boom out, "Round 'em up." I turned and saw Chief Tyler and his two goons standing on the beach near the trailhead. "Start with her," he said, pointing at Nancy.

That was a mistake. Even if the older women didn't have the strength to overpower the two goons, she'd give them a tongue-lashing they wouldn't soon forget.

"What do you think you're doing, young man?" she said, jabbing her long purple fingernails into the abdomen of the larger of the two men. "Does your mother know you're harassing old ladies? Is this how she raised you? Wait until I tell her about your behavior."

His brow furrowed as he took a step backwards. Clearly a mama's boy.

When the other guy tried to grab Nancy's hands and pull them behind her, she stepped on his foot, then whirled around. "And you," she said. "I remember you from Sunday school. Constantly getting in trouble. Last time you misbehaved, your mother took away your bike. Do you want that to happen again?"

Goon number two's shoulders slumped. I could picture what he must have looked like as a little boy. I kind of felt sorry for him. Having Nancy as your Sunday school teacher couldn't have been easy. But at least he should have felt grateful he only had to see her once a week. Imagine if she had been his elementary school teacher. Five days a week of Nancy the schoolmarm would be too much for anyone.

Confused, the two goons looked at the chief for guidance. He shook his head, then approached Nancy. "You're trespassing."

"No, we're not. This is public land."

"No. Private," he said.

"No. Public," she retorted.

"Private."

"Public."

I kind of liked this one-word dialog of Nancy's. Much better than her usual long diatribes full of citations of applicable rules and regulations.

Then she reverted to type. "This land is public as per section 714 of the land use code. It was designated as such in 1862 by Coconut Carl himself and ratified by the Kalverleifde Council in 1867. We have every right to be on this beach. Are we clear, dear?"

The chief was silent.

"I didn't hear you," she said.

He continued to stare at her impassively.

"Your mother was an Abbott, wasn't she?"

He narrowed his eyes.

She narrowed hers right back. "The Abbott family was known for their charitable donations to organizations who protect public lands such as these." She made a sweeping gesture at the beach. "They wanted the public to be able to enjoy beautiful nature spots like these, even people who aren't residents of Destiny Key. What would she think of you trying to chase us off this land?"

He folded his arms across his chest. "What's your point, lady?"

"The Coconut Cove Regatta has been anchoring in this bay and using this beach for as long as I remember, and it's going to stay that way. Understood?"

I was impressed with how Nancy was managing the situation. This was one of those times when her knowledge of rules and regulations, not to mention her stubbornness, was an advantage. She had the scrawny man under her thumb. I decided to take advantage of the situation and press the chief for answers to more concerning matters.

"Why are you covering up Gregor's murder?" I asked.

Nancy shushed me. "Let's stay focused on the issue at hand."

"The cover-up is the issue," I insisted. "He wants us off the island so we don't expose him."

Scooter grabbed my arm and pulled me back. "What are you doing? Nancy has this under control."

"He's going to get away with it," I said.

Ned whispered, "I thought we had agreed that it would be better to pretend it had been an accidental death."

"It wasn't an accident," I said loudly. "It was murder."

The chief stroked his chin. "Fine. We can play it your way. Mr. Smirnov was murdered."

"Great," I said. "Now you need to conduct a proper investigation. Go through the evidence, carry out an autopsy, and interview witnesses."

"The investigation has already been completed," he said.

"How could you have finished it already? Up until ten seconds ago you were claiming it was an accident."

"We're very efficient in Destiny Key." He gave me a cold smile. "So efficient, in fact, that I'm going to arrest the killer right now."

"But she's not here," I said.

"Of course she is," he replied, pointing at Anabel. "Take her into custody," he said to the two goons.

As they grabbed her, the chief looked at me and asked, "Happy now?"

CHAPTER 9
THE R2-D2 PENCIL HOLDER

We all stood in shock for a few moments, then I sprinted toward the path. "Come on, we have to go after them," I said over my shoulder.

Scooter raced up behind me and grabbed me by my waist. "Stop. Those guys have guns."

I tried to squirm out of his grasp, but he held me tight. "These goons are too intimidated by Nancy to use them," I said.

"They might be, but I don't think the chief would hesitate to draw his. You heard the stories about him. I don't want to see anyone get hurt, especially you." He turned me around so that I faced him and kissed me gently on the forehead.

"We need to call Chief Dalton and let him know what happened," I said.

The dispatcher was reluctant to put my call through, claiming that I wasted too much of the chief's time reporting UFO sightings. Then she hung up on me. It wasn't until my third attempt that I was able to spit out what had happened to

Anabel. She put me straight through after that.

"This better not be one of your calls asking the department to contribute to that organization of yours," he said gruffly.

"No, it's about the mother of your fur babies," I said impatiently. "We were on the beach having a picnic when Chief Tyler arrested her."

I held the phone away from my ear while he screamed a few choice words about Chief Tyler. Then I heard a loud crash, followed by a deep breath.

"What was that noise?" I asked.

"Something might have flown across the room," he said.

"I hope it wasn't that R2-D2 pencil holder I gave you."

"It wasn't. But that's a good idea," he said, followed by another loud crash.

"Chief, you need to focus," I said. "Breaking things isn't going to help."

"What I need to do is get Anabel back and wring Tyler's neck. How could you let this happen?"

"Me? It wasn't my fault," I said with a mixture of defiance and guilt. Had it been my fault that Chief Tyler was trying to pin Gregor's murder on her? Should I have tried harder to talk Nancy out of having a barbecue on the beach?

"I know it wasn't your fault," the chief said softly. "It's my fault. I shouldn't have let Anabel go to Destiny Key. Bad things happen there."

"I did try to stop them, but Scooter was worried someone would get shot. He wouldn't let me go after them."

"That was smart. He did the right thing. He was protecting his wife. Something I failed to do with mine." After a pause, he said, "I mean my ex-wife. Where are you now?"

"We're still on the beach."

"Who's 'we'?"

"Ned, Nancy, Scooter, Mrs. Moto and me. Everyone else already went back to their boats."

"I'm surprised that cat of yours didn't try to attack Tyler," the chief said. "She's been known to go after bad guys before."

"She was on the other side of the beach chasing lizards." I smiled as I watched Mrs. Moto try to persuade Nancy to pick her up. The older woman kept trying to shoo her away, but the calico persisted in rubbing against her legs.

"That's probably a good thing. Frick and Frack would never forgive me if anything happened to their friend. Okay, let me think." After a moment, he said, "Go back to your boat and wait by the phone. I'll call you later."

"What are you going to do?"

"Borrow my buddy's boat and get Anabel back," he said firmly.

I looked at the anchorage. The sun was starting to go down. When we had sailed over from Coconut Cove on the first day of the regatta, it had taken us hours. By the time Chief Dalton got here, Anabel would have been rotting in a cell for hours. When I explained as much to the chief and suggested that we might have to break her out of jail ourselves, he laughed.

"I'm not taking a sailboat. My buddy has a powerboat. It will take less than an hour to get from town to the public dock on Destiny Key. It's on the other side of the island from where you are. Besides, they don't have a jail on the island. Tyler will probably have her stowed away at the ferry terminal. He has an office there."

"Well, in that case, do you think we should head back to Coconut Cove tonight?" The thought of sailing in the dark terrified me, but if he thought we could do more good there, I'd swallow my fear.

"No, you stay there in case I need back-up."

"What about Chief Tyler? Do you think he'll come after us?"

"No way he'll try anything with all those boats anchored there. The only thing he cares about is getting you off Destiny Key."

"Doesn't that strike you as odd?" I asked. "I know they don't like strangers on the island, but his reaction seems to be a bit extreme."

"Everything about him is extreme. Look, I need to get going. I'll phone you later."

After the chief hung up, I explained the situation to the rest of the gang.

"Well, I, for one, will be glad to get off this island," Ned said. "We'll need to think about doing something differently for next year's regatta."

As we walked to the dinghy, Nancy said, "Do you need any help with the investigation?"

"Help? Investigation?" I said with surprise. "You were the one who told me in no uncertain words to drop it."

"That was before," she said.

"Before what?" I asked.

"Before that horrible man arrested your friend, dear. Sure, Anabel is ditzy, but she couldn't hurt a fly. We all know she's innocent. Now, you just have to prove it. It's about time the world knew what happens on this island."

"You know what this means, don't you?" I said. "I have to get Victoria to confess to what she did and turn herself in."

* * *

As Ned steered the dinghy toward *Marjorie Jane*, Mrs. Moto leaned over the edge and yowled.

"Do you think she wants to go swimming again?" Ned asked.

"I think that was her 'Where's my after-dinner snack' cry," Scooter said.

"I'm surprised that cat doesn't weigh more considering how much she eats," Nancy said.

"She gets a lot of exercise—spider squashing, lizard hunting, seagull chasing, and now swimming."

After Ned pulled alongside our boat, he said, "Call us the minute you hear anything from Chief Dalton."

"Will do," Scooter said as he lifted the admiral on deck.

Melvin and Ben were sitting in the cockpit playing cards. "You guys stayed at the beach for quite a while," the older man said.

"It's a long story," I said.

"Gin and tonic?" Scooter asked.

"Please. A large one," I said.

Melvin set his cards down. "What's going on? You look upset."

"He's right," Ben said. "You have that wrinkle thing between your eyebrows going on. The one you get when something's not right."

"Where's Victoria?" I asked.

"She's lying down," Ben said. "She said she has a headache coming on."

I rubbed my temples. "Yeah, I know how she feels."

Melvin looked around the cockpit. "Wait a minute. Where's Anabel?"

I sighed. "I don't even know where to begin. Let me have my drink first and then I'll fill you in."

After a few minutes, Scooter handed up bowls filled with pretzels, almonds, and potato chips. "The G&Ts are coming up. Melvin? Ben? Want one?"

Ben grabbed some nuts. "I'll take a beer if you have one."

"I wouldn't mind a G&T," Melvin said.

A voice behind Scooter said. "Ooh, gin and tonics. My favorite." Victoria pushed past Scooter and climbed into the cockpit. Ben scooted over to make room for her. "Can I have lemon in mine?"

"I thought you had a headache," I said. "Are you sure you should be drinking?"

"I did, but I took my magic pill and now it's gone. A gin will help make sure it stays away." Her eyes looked a little unfocused. I wondered exactly what kind of magic was in the pill she had taken.

"And now that you're a sailor, the lemon in your drink will help prevent scurvy," Ben joked.

After Scooter passed our drinks around, Melvin said, "So, tell us about Anabel. Where is she?"

Victoria looked around, perplexed. "What do you mean? Isn't Anabel here?"

"No, she's not," I said. "Chief Tyler arrested her."

"Arrested?" Melvin said. "For what?"

I fixed my gaze on Victoria to gauge her reaction before saying, "Gregor's murder."

She looked at me blankly, then squeezed lemon into her drink.

After we explained what happened, Ben said, "I should have stayed there with you. We could have overpowered them, right Scooter?"

"They had guns," he said defensively.

"You made the right call," I said, squeezing his arm. "That's what Chief Dalton said."

"I have a handgun for protection, but I don't know if I could ever use it," Victoria said. "They scare me."

"What about knives?" I asked.

Scooter whispered in my ear, "Real subtle."

I took another sip of my drink. "I'm way past subtle," I whispered back. Then, in a louder voice, I said, "Victoria, I'll put it on the line. You need to confess to Gregor's murder and turn yourself in."

The hazy look in her eyes vanished. She took a gulp of her drink. "I didn't murder Gregor."

"Yes you did. We have proof." I bit my lip. "Or at least we did."

"Proof?" she asked. "What proof?"

"Your hair," I said, looking at the long brown locks cascading down her back.

She put a hand up to the scarf she had tied around her head. "Why would my hair be proof?"

"Because we found it on Gregor's body."

She gave a brittle laugh. "Everyone has hair on their clothes. I probably have some of yours on mine and vice versa." She made a dramatic showing of plucking a hair off her shorts. "See."

"That's cat hair," I said.

"Humans shed just like cats," she said.

"This was different. It wasn't just a stray hair. It was a clump of hair. Gregor must have pulled it out during your struggle."

Her eyes got moist. "He didn't pull it out. It fell out. I have alopecia. My hair has been falling out. Why do you think I'm always wearing a hat or a scarf?"

"I figured it was your sense of style," I said.

"No, it's a disease. Not a fashion choice," she said angrily. She whipped her scarf off, twisted her head and pulled her hair up. She pointed at a bald patch. "See? My hair comes out in clumps."

"Oh." This was awkward. While she retied her scarf, I realized that the alopecia didn't explain everything. "We also found some strands of hair stuck in Gregor's signet ring. They were separate from the matted hair we found."

"He was stroking my head to help me fall asleep that night. It might have gotten caught then." Her eyes welled up. "It was a sweet moment together and my last memory of him alive."

"Hmm." I felt even more awkward. Not only had I made Victoria reveal her hair loss, I'd also made her cry.

"Was that your only evidence?" she asked.

"Well, there was the knife," I said reluctantly.

"It wasn't mine. The only knives I own are at home and I use them for eating, not killing people." She looked at her left hand as though imagining the engagement ring he had promised her. "We were going to be married. I wouldn't have killed him." After a beat, she held up her glass and shook it at Scooter. "How about another one?"

After my husband got us another round, Ben asked, "Well, if Victoria didn't do it, who did? It had to have been someone at Warlock's Manor. The road was cut off. No one else could have gotten there."

"That's a scary thought," Melvin said. "Kind of like that Agatha Christie novel. Which one was that again?"

"Oh, I know the one you mean. *Ten—*"

Ben interrupted. "Do you think we're all going to get knocked off one by one?"

"I don't think the killer is a homicidal maniac," I said. "Whoever killed Gregor had a specific motive. They're not going to go around randomly killing other people."

"Whatever you say, boss," Ben said, giving me a mock salute. "You have more experience in this area than the rest of us. So what do we do next?

"Well, there are only three other people who could have done it," I said.

"Three?" Victoria said. "I count six."

"How do you get six?" Scooter asked.

"There's Thomas, Sawyer, Olivia, and the three of you. That's six." She pointed at Melvin. "You stayed on *Marjorie Jane* so it wasn't you."

Melvin shifted uncomfortably on the seat.

"It wasn't us," I said.

"Says the woman who tried to pin the blame on me because I'm losing my hair," Victoria replied.

"I'm really sorry about that," I said. "But you can see how it looked."

"Ben has long brown hair. It could have been his," Victoria said.

"Tell you what, why don't we assume it wasn't him, me or Scooter. We didn't even know Gregor and there was an alarm system in the bunkhouse. It would have gone off if any of us had tried to leave."

"An alarm system?" Scooter said. "I didn't see one."

I pointed at the sleeping cat. "Her. If any of us had woken up, she would have screamed her head off to get her something to eat."

"True. That's an alibi that will hold up in court." Scooter smiled. "Can you imagine her testifying? She'd roll over and demand that the judge rub her belly."

"So that leaves Thomas, Olivia, and Sawyer," Melvin said. "Not that I ever believed any of you could have done it."

"It wasn't Thomas," Victoria said. "I've known him forever."

"I've known people forever who've ended up surprising me," I said.

"Why don't we put Thomas to the side for now?" Melvin said diplomatically. "What do you know about Sawyer and Olivia?"

Ben leaned forward. "It wasn't Sawyer. I've known her forever."

"So you're saying it was Olivia?" I asked Ben. "What motive could she have? She didn't know Gregor until this weekend. Sawyer at least knew who Gregor was." I gave Victoria a cautioning look. She seemed to understand what I meant and didn't say anything about Gregor and Sawyer having been romantically involved. The last thing I wanted was for Ben to get upset about Sawyer's love life, especially when the young woman had told me she only thought of her high-school classmate as a friend.

I also wasn't sure that what Victoria had said about the two of them was true. Gregor might have made up that story about dating Sawyer as a way of emotionally manipulating Victoria. But, on the other hand, Sawyer had changed the subject when I tried to ask her about her relationship with Gregor. Olivia had also mentioned something about how her friend liked older men, and Gregor had been way older than the young woman. Definitely something I would have to follow up on later.

"Did you hear me, Mollie?" Ben said. "It wasn't her."

I patted his hand. "I heard you." This whole conversation was going downhill. I was realizing that talking about suspects with friends of suspects was a bad idea. It was time to change the subject.

"So, what kind of costumes do you think Mrs. Moto should wear in her YouTube videos?"

It's amazing how talking about cats makes everyone chill out.

* * *

The next day was pretty eventful. Not eventful in terms of murder. No one else was killed, no one confessed, and no new evidence came to light. What was eventful was that *Marjorie Jane* won the final race back to Coconut Cove. Nancy claimed we cheated, and that I had to relinquish our trophy. I clutched the trophy to my chest and said something about sore losers. That rendered her speechless. I think she assumed that I was going to back down like the two goons had on the beach.

Fortunately, Ned intervened, reminding both of us that neither *Pretty in Pink* nor *Marjorie Jane* had won the overall regatta. Instead, that honor had gone to the catamaran, the *Mistletoe*. The couple that owned the boat were gracious winners, inviting all of us to a Christmas party on their boat. When I mentioned it was only July, and that December was a long way off, the wife laughed and told me it was never too early to start organizing catering. She seemed like the type of woman who filed her taxes early and never ran out of toilet paper.

That evening, Scooter and I met Anabel and Chief Dalton at the Tipsy Pirate. I was eager to hear more details about her escape from Destiny Key. When she had called me earlier, the brief update she had given sounded like something out of a James Bond movie, with the chief racing from Coconut Cove to the island in a powerboat, sneaking into the building where she was being held, and overpowering the goons standing guard, before whisking her back to the mainland. I had a feeling what really happened had probably been a little less exciting.

As we walked into the bar, I stopped to have a word with Coconut Carl's statue. "How come you never told me you were a ghost?" I asked. He didn't respond. Which is probably a good thing. When wooden statues start talking back, you've either had too many rum shots or something else weird is going on.

After I did the ritual rubbing of Carl's belly, Scooter asked me what I wished for. "To prove that Anabel is innocent."

"And...?" he prompted.

"And for Hershey's to start making S'mores candy bars again."

"Good call," he said. "I hope both of those wishes come true."

"What do you mean by 'you hope'? You don't think Anabel really did it, do you?"

"Of course not. It was just a figure of speech," Scooter said. He looked around the large room. The owners of the Tipsy Pirate had converted an old fish processing plant into a kitschy bar, popular with locals and tourists alike. There was still a lingering fishy odor, but after a few rum punches, people didn't seem to notice.

"Do you see them?" I asked.

"Yep. They're outside." As we walked over to join them, I noticed Frick and Frack sleeping quietly at the chief's feet. "We should have brought Mrs. Moto with us," I said.

Scooter looked over the railing of the back deck which extended out over the water. He pointed at some fish swimming past. "No way. She'd have dived in to go for a swim and make new friends."

I squinted in the Dalton's direction. "Do you notice anything different about the chief?"

Scooter shook his head.

"I think he trimmed his eyebrows. Guys do that sort of thing when there's a woman involved. He's trying to look good for Anabel."

"His eyebrows don't look any different to me," he said.

"They definitely do. It used to look like two giant caterpillars had taken up residence on his forehead. They were constantly twitching. It was like a form of sign language. I could tell what he was really thinking by looking at his bushy eyebrows. But now that they're neat and tidy, I don't have a clue."

Scooter laughed. "You're crazy. Let's go," he said, grabbing my hand.

As we neared the table, Anabel rushed over to me and gave me a hug.

"I'm so glad you're okay," I said.

"I'm fine now, thanks to Tiny." She beamed at her ex-husband. He gave her a shy smile in return.

"What can I get you?" a waitress asked after we had taken our seats.

After she returned with drinks and appetizers, the chief said he wanted to take our statements.

"Statements?" I said. "That seems quite formal. We're having egg rolls with pineapple dipping sauce. Hardly the type of food that goes with an interrogation."

The chief frowned. "I said a statement, not an interrogation."

"What kind of food do you think goes with an interrogation?" Anabel asked me.

"Something with mashed potatoes and gravy," I said. "You really need something that's going to stick to your ribs if the police are grilling you."

"Ladies, this isn't a cooking show," the burly man said

impatiently. "I need everyone to cooperate if we're going to clear Anabel's name."

"We have the same goal," I said soberly. "What do you need?"

Anabel placed her hand on the chief's arm. "Tiny needs your help."

"He does?" I said.

"He does." She looked at her ex. "Don't you? Tell her what you told me."

The chief jabbed an egg roll into the dipping sauce, splattering it across the table.

Anabel handed him a napkin, then said, "Why don't I just go ahead and tell you? We need you to find out who murdered Gregor. Tiny can't get officially involved. If he's caught poking his nose into things, it will cause trouble for him. So we want to hire you to be our private investigator."

The chief made a choking sound, then spluttered, "That's not what I said. What I said was that I wanted you to do what you do best—be a busybody."

I shrugged. "I can do that." After pulling a notebook out of my purse, I started making a list. "The first thing we need to do is make sure Gregor's body has a proper autopsy. Second is to get a hold of the evidence and have it analyzed by someone trustworthy."

"How are you going to get the evidence?" Scooter asked. "It's on Destiny Key."

"Let's put a pin in that and come back to it later," I said. "Third, we need to interview the suspects. And fourth..." I tapped my pen on the notebook. "What was the fourth thing?"

"It probably had something to do with chocolate," the chief said dryly.

"No, that's not it. But that is a good point." I jotted down, '4 - Buy more M&M'S.' "Okay, let's talk about the suspects—Thomas, Victoria, Olivia, and Sawyer. Let's cover their possible motives first, then talk about opportunity."

The chief bit back a smile. "Go on."

"I hate to say it," I said, pausing to make sure no one was listening in on our conversation, "but Thomas has the strongest motive. There was a lot of bad blood between the two of them. Then, when Gregor showed up uninvited and started acting like he owned the place, it might have been the straw that broke his back."

"Thomas is such a nice guy," Anabel said. "I can't picture him killing someone."

"We have to leave our emotion out of it," I said. "Next is Victoria. At first, I was convinced that she did it because of the hair that we found, but..." I looked at Anabel. "Did you know she was losing her hair?"

"No," she said. "But that might explain why she started wearing hats and scarves earlier this year. Poor thing."

"Uh-huh. From what she told us, it explains how the hair ended up in the dinghy and how it was caught in Gregor's ring."

"So, you're ruling her out because she had a convincing explanation," the chief said.

I sat back in my chair. "That's a good point. Even if her hair fell out in their room that night, she still could have lost some during an altercation with Gregor. You're pretty good at this," I said.

He snorted. "That must be why they gave me a badge."

"Have I shown you this?" I reached into my purse and pulled out a leather wallet. I flipped it open to reveal an identification card and a badge with a spaceship logo. "See, it's from FAROUT. It proves that I'm an official investigative reporter."

The chief put his head in his hands. "Can we get back to the suspects, please?"

"Okay. Let's move onto Sawyer. Victoria told us that Gregor was having an affair with her. He broke it off, and she got upset."

The chief nodded. "Jealously is often a motive."

"The thing is that I'm not sure whether it's true or not." I turned to Scooter. "I thought we could invite Sawyer over for dinner tomorrow night. We can say it's so that she can see the inside of *Marjorie Jane* since she made those nice sketches of the outside. Then we can grill her about her love life."

"What are you thinking of making?" he asked.

"Lasagna," I said. "Italian food and a nice bottle of red wine is the perfect recipe for an investigative session."

"Chianti would be nice," Scooter said. "Will there be garlic bread too?"

"Okay, enough chit-chat about your dinner menu," the chief said. What about the other girl, Olivia?"

"She didn't know Gregor at all," I said. "I can't see a motive."

"Those are the ones you have to look at more closely," the chief said.

"Fair enough. Scooter can question her."

Scooter set down his glass on the table. "Me? I'm not the busybody, you are." When he saw the look on my face, he clarified. "I meant investigator, not busybody. I wouldn't know where to begin."

"I'll give you a list of questions and prep you," I said. "You have the perfect excuse to speak with her."

"I do?" he asked.

"Sure," I said. "You can talk to her about your YouTube channel, then casually direct the conversation to the murder."

"You seem to have this under control," Anabel said to me before turning to Chief Dalton. "Doesn't she, honey?"

He pursed his lips, probably to keep a compliment about me from escaping them. "So you have plans to question the two girls. What about Thomas and Victoria?"

"Thomas is easy. We'll go for breakfast at the Sailor's

Corner Cafe tomorrow and catch him there. He said he would be hanging some new paintings for sale."

"And Victoria?" the chief asked.

After a moment, I said, "I know. She left her hat on our boat. I'll go return it and have a chat with her."

"What about opportunity?" Anabel asked. "We've talked about motive, but not opportunity."

"Good point," I said. "Sawyer and Olivia shared a room. Could one of them have sneaked out in the middle of the night without the other one knowing?"

Anabel shrugged. "Maybe. It depends if the other one was a heavy sleeper."

"Thomas had his own room, so it wouldn't have been a problem for him to have gone downstairs without anyone noticing." I eyed the lone egg roll on the plate. Before I could make my move, Scooter swiped it. I gave him a look, then continued, "But Victoria and Gregor were sharing a room. Did she lure him down to the dock somehow to kill him there? Were they out for a stroll, got into an argument and then she stabbed him?"

The chief cleared his throat. "Any one of them had opportunity. I suggest you focus on motive." His phone buzzed. "I need to get this."

While the chief was chatting, the rest of us debated whether we should order more egg rolls or try the fried cheese balls. I suggested we get both.

"I've got some bad news."

I looked up from the menu.

Chief Dalton's face looked grim. "You can cross the first item off your list. There won't be an autopsy. Gregor was buried at sea this afternoon."

CHAPTER 10
EDWARD SCISSORHANDS

The next morning, Scooter and I went to the Sailor's Corner Cafe to speak with Thomas. As usual, people were lined up outside patiently waiting for a table. Conversation buzzed as everyone shared how they had spent the Fourth of July weekend. Parades, fireworks, and picnics topped their lists. I decided not to mention that we had celebrated with sparklers and a murder investigation.

When we finally got inside I was surprised by how chaotic things were. Customers were impatiently waiting to pay their checks, dirty dishes were piled up on tables, and the cook was pounding on the bell in the kitchen.

"Order up," he yelled. "Is anyone out there? Food's getting cold!"

As we waited to be seated, Jim rushed past balancing a tray with one hand and carrying a pot of coffee in the other. While he was topping up a young couple's coffee cups, their toddler wriggled in his high chair, knocking a glass of juice on the floor. The harried man let out an exasperated sigh, then bent down to clean up the mess.

An older man shouted from across the room. "We've been waiting for over an hour. Where's our order?"

Jim placed the broken glass and the wet rag in a bin at the service station, straightened his Hawaiian shirt, then smiled at the man. "Coming right up, sir." It was one of those smiles that looks slightly manic, like a nervous breakdown could happen at any minute.

We caught Jim's eye as he walked toward the kitchen. "Sit anywhere you like," he muttered.

Fortunately for us, our favorite booth had just opened up. Unfortunately for Jim, it was because the couple who had been waiting to order got fed up and stormed out.

I grabbed a couple of menus from the hostess station and passed one to Scooter as we sat down. "What are you going to get?" I asked, although I knew the answer. He always ordered a Denver omelet and hash browns. Pancakes with extra-crispy bacon was my usual.

Scooter checked the time on his phone. "Do you see Thomas anywhere around here?" he asked. "I have a conference call in an hour."

I scanned the room. The cafe was decorated with arts and crafts for sale. I noticed a few paintings that obviously were Anabel's—the unicorns, fairies, and dragons were a giveaway. There were a couple of drawings of sailboats on the far wall. I wondered if they were Sawyer's work. Prominently displayed near the entrance were Thomas' paintings. A display of greeting cards, carved model ships, and jewelry was positioned next to the cash register.

"No, I don't see him," I said. "Maybe he's helping out in the kitchen."

After a few minutes, Jim came to take our order. "Sorry, folks. Alejandra is out of town, and two of the other waitresses called in sick."

"Where's Alejandra?" Scooter asked.

"She's at a cosmetology convention," he said.

"I told you about that," I reminded Scooter. "She texted yesterday to say that it's going really well. She's lined up suppliers and ordered a couple of pedicure spa chairs."

"Oh, yeah. Her nail salon is opening soon," Scooter said.

"Uh-huh," I said. "She leased a space at the Seaside Center. She's nervous about the grand opening."

"I'm sure it will be fine." He wagged a finger at me. "As long as you don't stumble across another murder."

"A murder at a nail salon," I said. "Don't be ridiculous."

Jim looked up from his phone. "Phew. One of the gals is going to be able to take a shift. She should be here in about thirty minutes." He surveyed the room. "Hopefully, I can keep the crowd under control until then."

The bell rang again. "Order up."

"Do you need help?" Scooter asked. "My little stegosaurus used to waitress part-time back in Cleveland."

Jim's eyes lit up. "Really? Do you think you could help out?"

"Happy to," I said.

"Thanks." He breathed a sigh of relief. "Breakfast is on me."

"With extra bacon?" I asked.

He smiled and handed me an apron. "As much as you can eat."

Scooter grinned. "You'll be sorry you said that."

After taking orders, filling coffee cups, and bussing tables for a half hour, I remembered why I never became a professional waitress. My feet were killing me. Finally, the other waitress arrived and took over for me.

As I slid into the booth, Scooter held up his coffee mug. "Refill?"

"No way," I said.

"You're not going to get a tip with an attitude like that," he joked.

As the breakfast crowd thinned out, Jim set our orders in front of us. "Extra bacon, as promised. Plus extra butter for those pancakes. I think you've earned those calories. Can I get you anything else?"

"Why don't you have a seat and rest a while?" I pointed at the waitress. "It looks like she has things under control."

I scooted over in the booth and Jim slid in next to me.

"We were hoping to see Thomas here," Scooter said.

"He's at Coconut Creations," Jim said.

"Gregor's gallery?" I asked. "What's he doing there?"

"It's top secret," Jim said with a smile.

"A good kind of secret or a bad kind?" I asked.

"A very good kind. He's had some good luck. I'll let him tell you about it."

Scooter took a sip of coffee. "After what happened on Destiny Key, he could use some good luck."

Jim frowned. "You're telling me. He hardly slept a wink last night. He was tossing and turning."

"Bad dreams about the murder?" I asked.

"Yes. It upset him on a number of levels," Jim stroked his white beard. "First finding the body and then the altercation with Chief Tyler. But the straw that broke the camel's back was finding out Anabel had been arrested."

"Finding the body?" Scooter said. "But Mollie found Gregor."

Jim looked flustered. "I meant seeing the body. I can't imagine going through something like that. How do you do it, Mollie?"

I shrugged. "I've never really thought about it."

"I'm just glad he got off that god-awful island," Jim said. "Did you know it's haunted? Terrible things happen there. It's not the first murder that's taken place there."

I leaned forward. "Really?"

"Did you ever hear about Coconut Carl?" Jim asked.

"Oh, that. I don't think that had anything to do with

Gregor," I said. "What exactly was the beef Thomas had with him?"

"Oh, that's right," Jim said. "I forgot the two of you are relatively new to Coconut Cove and don't know all the scuttlebutt. Thomas used to own an art gallery in town. Then Gregor arrived and put him out of business."

"He took over Thomas' gallery, right?" I asked.

Jim nodded.

"That seems odd. I would have thought that this town is big enough for two galleries. There are plenty of tourists with money to spend."

"That should have been the case, but that just goes to show you what a petty man Gregor was," Jim said. "He wanted to run the only gallery in town. He pressured local artists to stop exhibiting at the gallery when Thomas owned it."

"How did he manage that?" I asked. "From what I know, Thomas is a respected member of the local art community. Why wouldn't his fellow artists want to support him?"

"Partly through spreading rumors about Thomas and partly through blackmail." He fussed with the ketchup and mustard bottles. "The worst was when he accused Thomas of embezzlement. He sent a letter to the newspaper claiming that Thomas didn't pay artists their full commissions. And the editor had the audacity to print it. Thomas made his financial records available to anyone who wanted to see them, but the damage was already done. Then Gregor swooped in and made Thomas a low-ball offer for the gallery. He was deep in the red by that point and didn't have any choice but to accept it."

"Wow, that takes a lot of guts," Scooter said.

"It does. But that's the kind of guy Gregor was. He was a bully, but a charismatic one. People wanted to believe him because he was well known in the international art world. I think they hoped some of his fame would rub off of them."

"You mentioned blackmail," I said.

"Yeah, for those folks that didn't play ball based on

rumors, Gregor threatened to expose secrets he knew about them. That's how he got Victoria on his side."

"What kind of hold did he have on Victoria?" I asked.

"I don't know," Jim said. "All I know is that Thomas overheard Victoria and Gregor talking one evening. Gregor threatened to expose her unless she stuck with him. Thomas spoke with her about it later and tried to convince her not to give in to blackmail, but she told him she didn't have a choice."

"After the way he treated her, it's really hard to believe that she ended up dating Gregor," Scooter said.

"I know," Jim agreed. "I think that's why she kept it secret from everyone. She only told Thomas about their relationship after she and Gregor had a fight."

"Did anyone stand up to him?" I asked.

"A few. Anabel was one of them. I don't think Gregor could find anything to blackmail her with, so he went to his next favorite tactic—attacking her reputation. He had one of his cronies write a scathing review about her work in an art journal. Anabel's business was cut nearly in half. She's recovered since then, but it was a huge blow at the time." Jim gestured around the cafe at the artwork on display. "Gregor is the reason why you see all of this here. We started displaying Thomas' work, along with work by other artists who defied Gregor."

Scooter's phone buzzed. "Sorry. I need to get going or I'll be late for my conference call."

"I should get back to work too," Jim said as he stood. "Thanks for helping out, Mollie. If you ever want to pick up any shifts, all you have to do is ask."

After Jim walked over to talk with the waitress, I leaned across the table. "Remember what he said about Thomas finding Gregor's body?"

"Yeah, but he said he meant seeing him," Scooter said.

"Well, here's what I'm wondering—assuming Thomas

didn't murder Gregor, did he discover the body before I did? If so, what was he doing out at the dock?" I drummed my fingers on the table. "Next stop—Coconut Creations for some answers."

* * *

After I dropped Scooter at the marina for his conference call, I headed to the gallery. As I pulled into the gravel parking lot, I admired the whimsical topiaries dotting the grounds. How anyone could sculpt a living plant with hedge clippers into a remarkably accurate depiction of Goldilocks and the Three Bears was beyond me. I had tried cutting my own hair with nail scissors once. The goal had been a cute pixie cut. Instead, I ended up looking like Herman Munster. Imagine what I'd do to a plant if I tried to go all Edward Scissorhands on it.

When I walked up the pathway to the building, I noticed a large Coconut Creations sign propped against the wall. Gregor's name had been covered with red spray paint and his trademark symbol had been crossed out.

As I entered the gallery, Thomas was talking on his phone. His outfit was more sedate than usual. He wore gray pants and a white shirt. The only pops of color were his red beret, striped bow tie, and yellow duckie cuff links.

"How long will it take to print new ones?" he asked, grabbing a stack of brochures from the reception desk. "Can you make it a rush order? It should say, 'The Thomas Sinclair Coconut Creations Art Gallery.' Get rid of any references to Gregor." After a pause, he continued. "Okay, thanks. I'll pick them up later today."

As he tossed the brochures into a trashcan, one fluttered to the ground. He picked it up, then tore it into tiny pieces, muttering something about 'the Russian devil' under his breath.

I coughed to get his attention. He whirled around. "Oh,

Mollie. I didn't see you standing there."

"I just walked in. It's my first time here." I looked at the old ticket booth next to the entryway. "I love how they transformed this old railway station."

He rubbed his hands together. "It will look better after..." His voice trailed off as he smiled slyly.

"After what?" I prompted.

His smile grew. "If I tell you, can you promise to keep it a secret?" He didn't wait for my reply before continuing. "I'm so excited. I have to tell someone or else I'll burst. I'm buying back the gallery!"

"You are? Congratulations. When did this happen?"

"Last night. I spoke with Gregor's widow to offer my condolences."

I scowled. "Not really a surprise that the rat was married." Thomas nodded. "Well, I guess that was nice of you to call her, considering..." I hesitated.

"Considering what?" Thomas asked.

"Well, it's just that you weren't exactly a fan of Gregor's."

"I wasn't," he said. "But etiquette is still important. We ended up talking for an hour. She lives in New York and doesn't want to own a gallery in Florida. She was happy to get rid of this place for a bargain price. Even less than Gregor paid me when he stole it from me."

"Wow. Why would she do that?" I asked.

He shrugged. "She said that Coconut Cove is too parochial for her."

"Sounds like a snob," I said.

"Agreed. But, as long as she's willing to sell, she can turn up her nose at our little town all she likes."

"Has the sale gone through already?"

"No, but we agreed to the deal in principle," Thomas said. "It will take the lawyers a few days to finalize everything and transfer ownership from the holding company to me. In the meantime, she said I can start making changes."

"I noticed the sign outside. Was that your handiwork with the spray paint?"

Thomas' face reddened. "It was a bit childish."

"Understandable, after the way Gregor treated you." I looked at the dark circles under his eyes. "I saw Jim at the cafe this morning. He said that you hadn't slept well."

"No, I didn't get much sleep. Too excited about the gallery."

"That's what kept you up? Not the murder? I had a nightmare last night about finding Gregor's body."

"Of course, that played a part too," he said, looking down at the floor. "I didn't mean to sound callous."

"But you're glad he's dead." I waved my hand around the gallery. "If he hadn't have been killed, you wouldn't have this."

"It's no secret that I didn't like the man." He pounded the desk with his fist. "And, yeah, I'm glad he's dead."

I took a step back.

"Sorry. I didn't mean to scare you. It's just the lack of sleep. It's made me edgy."

I thought about what Thomas had said. Was it a strategic move on his part to act happy about Gregor's death? Did he think that threw suspicion off of him?

"Did Gregor have other enemies?" If Thomas was the killer, I was curious where he would try to shift the blame.

He fiddled with his cuff links. "I don't know if I should say."

"Go on," I said, crossing my fingers behind my back. "I can keep a secret."

He took a deep breath. "Well, Anabel hated Gregor. She had her lawyer send him a letter threatening to sue for defamation of character. When provoked, she can have quite the temper. She always jokes that it has something to do with her red hair. But maybe she let her temper get the better of her."

I bit my lip. It was true that Anabel could be hotheaded. I had even been on the receiving end of one of her angry letters before we became friends. Was I letting my feelings for her get in the way of seeing things clearly?

No, it couldn't have been her, I told myself. I shoved my hands in my pockets and said, "A lawsuit and murder are quite different things. Do you really think she did it?"

He held up his hands. "It's not my place to say."

"Why not? You've known her longer than I have. In fact, you know everyone who could have done it—Victoria, Sawyer, and Olivia."

"I don't know Olivia well," he said. "The first time I met her was when she gave her YouTube seminar. Come to think of it, what do we know about her besides her public persona? She's a stranger. Maybe you should focus your attention on her. You can speak with her tomorrow at the reception."

"The reception?" I asked.

"Oh, didn't I say? I'm having a small gathering to celebrate getting my gallery back. You and Scooter should come." He held up his phone. "I hope you don't mind. I have some more calls to make. Feel free to have a look around. There's a nice collection of miniature watercolors in the next room. They make great gifts."

The watercolors weren't really my cup of tea. They all featured different pink flowers—tea roses, carnations, peonies, and hydrangeas. Penny's birthday was coming up. The paintings were small enough that she might have room to hang one in her sailboat. As I went into the main room to ask Thomas how much the one of the camellias cost, I heard him on the phone.

"Sawyer, it's Thomas. Great news. I'm the new owner of Coconut Creations. How would you like to come work here again?" After a pause, he laughed. "I promise, I'll be a far better boss than Gregor ever was."

I tucked myself back around the corner and leaned against

the wall. Sawyer was on thin ice claiming that she didn't really know Gregor. Sure, maybe she hadn't been having an affair with him like Victoria claimed, but you can hardly work for a man and say that you're just acquaintances. Dinner conversation was going to be very interesting. I suddenly had a lot more questions to ask her.

CHAPTER 11
OREO COOKIES AND MILK

I slipped out of the gallery and headed to my next interview of the day. It was time to turn the heat up on Victoria.

She lived in an apartment tucked away in a quiet lane behind Penelope's Sugar Shack. Many of the buildings in Coconut Cove were painted in bright tropical colors, and Victoria's was no exception—turquoise wooden siding, lemon yellow shutters, and fuchsia trim. As I climbed the stairs to the second floor, I rehearsed the questions I wanted to ask.

"Did you see Gregor get up in the middle of the night and leave your room?"

"Did you know that Gregor's cane had a hidden knife?"

"Did you know Gregor was married?"

And, of course, "Are you sure you didn't kill Gregor? Maybe it slipped your mind? Totally understandable if it did. I'm a complete ditz that way too. I went all the way to the grocery store last week and completely forgot what I went there to buy. I stood there for ten minutes, then just ended up buying some Oreo cookies. It wasn't until I got back to the boat that I remembered that I was supposed to buy milk. Which was a shame as there's nothing better than dunking Oreos into a glass of milk."

By the time I got to the top of the stairs, my stomach was growling. I promised it that we'd get something to eat after speaking with Victoria. Then I knocked on the door. When I didn't get a response, I banged louder. After the third time, a voice called out, "Go away. I don't want what you're selling."

I leaned against the door. "It's me, Mollie. I'm not here to sell anything. I'm just returning your hat."

"Just leave it on the doormat," she said.

I looked down at the coir mat. It had "Please go away" printed on it. Personally, I don't think doormats should try to boss you around. So, I rattled the doorknob. "Victoria, please let me in. I'd rather not leave your hat outside. A raccoon might come by and grab it."

"How would a raccoon get in the building?" Victoria asked.

"They're very devious creatures," I said. "They'd probably get one to stand on another one's shoulders so that he could pick the lock. With those little hands of theirs they'd crack it open in no time. I had to press all the buttons until someone would buzz me in. It took forever." I tapped on the door. "So, what do you say? Are you going to let me in?"

I heard the sound of several deadbolts being unlocked. Then the door started to open. When I tried to push on it, I discovered that Victoria had left the chain attached. As she slipped her hand through the crack, her wrist brace caught on the latch. She pulled it free, then told me to hand the hat to her.

"Do you have a few minutes?" I asked after she pulled it through the door.

"No. I'm not feeling well," she said between coughs.

"Can I get you anything?" I offered.

"No thanks. I just need to go back to bed." As the door started to close, I called out, "Will we see you at the reception at the art gallery tomorrow?"

She didn't respond, so I heeded the doormat's wishes and left.

Next, I popped into the Sugar Shack for a latte and a couple of oatmeal cookies. While I walking back to my car, Chief Dalton phoned to ask me to meet him at the marina patio as soon as possible. I agreed. Before he hung up, he added, "Don't tell Anabel."

As I nibbled on one of the cookies, I wondered what it was that he didn't want me to tell her. Was he planning a surprise party for her? Or was he going to ask her to marry him again and wanted my advice on how to propose? I was so excited to find out what the chief had up his sleeve that I accidentally dropped my other cookie on the sidewalk. A seagull swooped down and snatched it away.

When I got to the patio, the chief was pacing back and forth. "What took you so long?" he asked when he saw me.

I held up a bag. "I had to get more cookies. Don't worry, I got some for you too. Have you thought about having Penelope do the catering for the reception?"

As we sat at one of the tables, he asked, "What reception?"

"The wedding reception, silly," I said. "Do you want chocolate chip or oatmeal?"

"Who's getting married?"

"You are," I said, still holding the cookies in my hand.

"What are you talking about? I'm not getting married."

"Really?" I set the cookies on a napkin and placed them in front of the chief. "Anabel will be disappointed."

He looked stunned. "She will?" Then he shook his head. "This is another one of your crazy tangents, isn't it? We need to focus on what's important—Anabel."

"I thought that's what we were doing," I said, eyeing up the uneaten cookies.

He placed his hands flat on the table and took a deep breath. "Normally, you'd be the last person I'd talk to about this, but—"

"Gee, thanks. Don't I feel special?"

"That's not what I meant." He picked at one of the cookies. "I don't know who I can trust these days."

"Well, you can trust me," I said. "Go on, spill it."

"I found out that Gregor was blackmailing Anabel."

"That doesn't make sense," I said. "Thomas told me that Gregor didn't have anything on her."

"He didn't until recently." The burly man rubbed his jaw, then started picking at the cookie again. "About two weeks ago, he emailed her an old picture."

"A picture of what?" I asked. "And for goodness sake, would you just eat that cookie already and stop plucking raisins out of it?"

He shrugged, then wolfed it down in two bites.

"See, sugar helps. Now tell me about the picture."

"A few years ago, Anabel was protesting medical testing on animals. She sneaked in a lab and 'liberated' some dogs," he said, making air quotes with his fingers. "Someone took a picture of her running out of the lab, a dog under each of her arms. If she didn't do what he wanted, Gregor threatened to get the picture published in the local newspaper."

I sat back in my chair. "I don't get it. Anabel is a hippie-chick, free-spirit kind of gal, right? She'd be proud of that picture. She's always protesting something. Just last week, I saw her outside the bowling alley holding up a sign—"

The chief held up his hand. "True. If it was just about her, she wouldn't have cared, but..." He shook his head as his voice trailed off.

I gasped. "Don't tell me. The dogs she rescued. Did they happen to be two Yorkshire terriers?"

He nodded.

"And are the dogs named Frick and Frack by any chance? The dogs the two of you share joint custody of?"

"Yes. She was trying to protect me," he said. "If anyone

found out I was harboring stolen dogs, it could be the end of my career. So she agreed to his demand."

I passed him another cookie. "What did he want?"

"She was supposed to write an article for an art journal praising Gregor and talking about the invaluable contribution he has made to the art world. He told her to send it to him by Saturday."

"This Saturday?"

The chief took a deep breath. "No, last Saturday. When she was at the artists' retreat..."

"The day Gregor turned up at Warlock's Manor," I said, finishing his sentence. "I see where this is going. Anabel had a strong motive to kill Gregor."

"Exactly."

"Don't worry. We'll figure this out. I already have some promising leads." I filled the chief in on the new developments while he nibbled on the last cookie. "Sawyer is my prime suspect now. She definitely knew Gregor, she had a grudge against him—either because he fired her or because he broke up with her or both—and she has some serious knife skills."

"You could say the same thing about Anabel," the chief said reluctantly.

"She has knife skills?" I asked.

"Yep. When we first got engaged, I taught her all sorts of self-defense techniques, including basic knife moves. She was really good at it."

"Well, that's not very helpful," I said. "I guess I just need to get Sawyer to confess."

The chief leaned forward. "This isn't one of these murder mystery shows you always watch. Murderers don't blurt out confessions. Convictions happen because of thorough investigations by trained professionals."

"We don't really have a choice, do we? There's no body." I paused and looked at the chief. "Hey, wait a minute, since there isn't a body, how can they convict Anabel?"

"If this had happened any place normal, instead of on Destiny Key, you'd have a point," he said. "But Tyler will find a way to make it stick. He's very well connected with people in positions of power."

I chewed on my lip for a moment. "Okay. We don't have a body, and goodness knows what happened to the evidence. It seems like everyone and their mother has a motive, opportunity, and the ability to have killed Gregor. Getting a confession seems like the simplest option at this point." I smiled. "Besides, it won't be the first time I've managed to get a killer to spill their guts."

The chief put his head in his hands and groaned. "I can't believe Anabel's fate depends on you getting Sawyer to confess."

"Piece of cake." I pushed my chair back from the table. "Now, I better get back to *Marjorie Jane* and start cooking. You know what they say, ply someone with good food and drink and they'll tell you all their secrets." As I walked past the chief, I put my hand on his shoulder. "You know, you really should tell Anabel how you feel about her."

He nodded. "Maybe. When this is all over."

* * *

"Permission to come aboard?" Sawyer asked as she knocked on *Marjorie Jane's* hull.

I leaned over the side of the cockpit. "Well, ordinarily I would give your permission, but I'm not the highest ranking member of this crew." I smiled and pointed at Mrs. Moto. "It's really up to the admiral."

At the sound of her name, the calico jumped out of my lap and bounded over to Sawyer.

"I think I know how to win her over." The young woman pulled a bag of cat treats out of her backpack. She set a few down on the deck and watched as the cat inhaled them. Mrs. Moto then sat back on her haunches and made a chirping sound.

"I think that means you can come aboard," I said.

After Sawyer climbed on board, she handed me a bottle of wine. "And here's a little something for you and Scooter."

"Thanks. That was sweet of you. This will be perfect with dinner." I patted a cushion next to me. "Have a seat. Scooter will be back any minute. While we're waiting, can I get you anything to drink? Soda? Gin and tonic?"

"A G&T would be great," she said. "Victoria said that you guys make good ones."

"Did she?" I asked, remembering how she had gulped them down when we were anchored at Destiny Key. "Did you see her recently?"

"Uh-huh. This afternoon at Coconut Creations."

"I was there today, as well," I said. "It was my first time there. It's a really lovely spot."

"Thomas did a great job renovating the building when he first bought it." Sawyer chuckled as Mrs. Moto tried to burrow in her backpack. "I think she wants more treats."

The admiral squawked as I pulled her out. "She can wait until after dinner." As I set the cat down, I said. "So why were you at the gallery today?"

Sawyer grinned. "Thomas offered me a part-time job. It's perfect. I'll work there a few days a week and focus on my art the rest of the time."

"Have you ever worked at an art gallery before?" I asked innocently.

"Uh-huh. In New York."

I cocked my head to the side. "Nowhere else?"

She shifted uncomfortably. Maybe it was because Mrs. Moto was kneading her legs with her claws slightly extended. Or maybe it was because she hadn't been forthright about working for Gregor. "Actually, I worked at Coconut Creations for a short while," she admitted.

"When Thomas owned it?"

"Uh, no. After he sold it."

"So you did know Gregor," I said casually.

"Oh, well, yeah. I didn't really know him on a personal level. It was a manager-employee relationship." She stroked the cat's fur. "I love this bobtail she has. It's so cute. Like a bunny rabbit."

"Shush. Don't say that too loudly. It will go to the admiral's head," I said. "I'd love to hear more about what it's like to work at an art gallery."

She stroked Mrs. Moto nervously. "Uh, well—"

"Ahoy there, ladies," Scooter said as he climbed on board. Sawyer seemed relieved by the interruption. He looked at the calico. "I think she wants your attention."

The admiral was nudging Sawyer's hand with her face, showing her exactly where she wanted to be petted. The young woman obediently scratched behind her ears.

"What's that in your hands?" I asked, eyeing the purple bakery box.

"I stopped by Penelope's to pick up dessert," he said.

"This is a great day for surprises." I held up the bottle. "First, Sawyer brought this and now you've brought a cake." I slid off the bench seat. "Hand me the box and I'll put it downstairs with the wine."

"How about some G&Ts while you're down there, my little stegosaurus?" Scooter said.

"Of course. I promised Sawyer one, but then we got to gabbing and I completely forgot."

Over cocktails, I tried to steer the conversation back to Sawyer's relationship with Gregor, but Scooter was oblivious to what I was trying to do. Instead, he happily chatted away about the latest dinosaur documentary he had seen. I honestly couldn't tell if she was genuinely interested in learning that "Micropachycephalosaurus" is the longest dinosaur name and that it means "tiny thick-headed lizard." She might have been fascinated or she might have just been a good actress, like when she told me on the beach that she didn't know Gregor.

After we finished our drinks, I suggested we go down below for dinner. "I have a lasagna in the oven. It should be ready in about ten minutes," I said. "There's also a tossed salad so we don't feel guilty about eating cake for dessert."

While I cut some Italian bread to go with our meal, Sawyer did some quick sketches of the interior of the boat. "I love that old oil lamp. It has such character." She set her charcoal pencil down and stood to get a closer look. When Mrs. Moto batted the pencil onto the floor, Scooter apologized, then bent under the table to retrieve it.

"Ouch," he said as he banged his head. He surfaced with the pencil, a toy mouse, and a crumpled up piece of paper. He held out the pencil to Sawyer, put the paper on the table, then tossed the mouse across the floor. Mrs. Moto bounded after it.

"Good. That should distract her for a while," I said, listening to the sound of her knocking it around in the aft cabin. "Dinner's ready." I set the casserole dish on the table. "Help yourself," I said, handing Sawyer a spatula while Scooter poured wine.

"Yum. This is delicious," Sawyer said after she took a bite.

"The secret is to layer basil leaves on top of the ricotta cheese mixture," I said. "The other secret is to wear pants with an elastic waistband because this isn't exactly low-cal. Not that you need to worry about that. You're young."

There was a lull in conversation while we ate. The only sound was that of the cat pouncing on her toy mouse. After taking a sip of wine, I said, "It seems a bit strange to be eating lasagna in July when it's almost one hundred degrees outside. We should be having something cold like pasta salad or gazpacho."

"That's what air conditioning is for," Scooter said as he helped himself to another slice of bread.

"Are you going to be able to cope without air conditioning when you go cruising full-time?" Sawyer asked.

I looked at Scooter. "What have you been telling her?"

Sawyer raised her eyebrows. "I thought you were going to sail around the world like Olivia."

"One of us thinks we're going to sail around the world," I said. "That wouldn't be me."

"She's not totally on board with the idea, but I'm working on her," Scooter said with a smile. "Admit it," he said to me. "You enjoyed our first cruise."

"Someone was killed," I said.

"Well, besides that," he replied. "The weather was great."

"Not on Destiny Key," I said.

"Okay, but besides that," he said. "We got to watch dolphins, and we won one of the races. Best of all, we didn't break anything. Think of how much money we saved."

"Are you forgetting the fact that our dinghy is still stuck on the island?" I asked. "We might have to buy a new one."

"That might be for the best," he said. "I'm not sure I want that one back."

As I patted Scooter's arm to reassure him, my hand brushed against the crumpled up paper he had set on the table. "What is this anyway?" I asked as I smoothed it out. "Oh yeah. Now I remember. It's a note that Nancy left taped to our boat reminding us to only use American quarters in the washing machine and dryer. Canadian and Bahamian coins are not acceptable. I crumpled it up for Mrs. Moto to play with it. Nancy would probably be upset if she knew I turned her note into a cat toy. She'd say that I wasn't taking it seriously enough. See how she put 'not' in capital letters and underlined it?" I asked Scooter.

He peered at the note, then pointed at the bottom paragraph. "What does 'N3V3R' mean?"

"Not sure. Looks like a typo." I held the paper up to the light for a better look. "Or maybe it's a code."

Scooter smirked. "A code? Do you think Nancy is some sort of spy?"

"Hang on a minute. This reminds me of something." I went into the aft cabin and dug through the bag we had with us on Destiny Key. As I returned to the table, I said, "I found this note in the shed by Warlock's Manor. It looks like it's written in some sort of code. Do you remember how I told you that Chief Tyler went into the shed and carried out bags to his vehicle?" Scooter nodded. "I thought he might have dropped this when he was in there."

"What was in the bags?" Sawyer asked.

"I'm not sure," I said. "But if I had to bet money on it, I would say it was something illegal. Chief Tyler is as crooked as they come. Maybe this note was about what he was supposed to steal. They put it in code so no one would be able to read it."

Scooter pointed at the torn edge. "You only have part of the note. Maybe that's why you can't understand it. It might not be code at all."

"Can I see it?" Sawyer asked.

"Sure." After I passed it to her, I topped up our wine glasses.

Sawyer took a sip of the Chianti, then said, "I don't think this is a code. I think it might be written in Cyrillic. See how this letter looks like a backwards 'N' and this one looks like the Greek letter phi?"

I furrowed my brow as I studied the piece of paper. "Where do they speak Cyrillic?"

"Cyrillic isn't a language. It's an alphabet. You know, like Russians use."

"I didn't think Chief Tyler was Russian," Scooter said.

"No, but Gregor was," I said. "So the question is, did Gregor write this note and, if so, what does it say?"

CHAPTER 12
SNOW WHITE AND THE SEVEN DWARFS

"This place it pretty cool," Scooter said as we pulled into the art gallery's parking lot.

"Wait until you see the topiaries," I said. "They're all fairy-tale themed."

"There's a free spot," Scooter pointed out as he drove to the rear of the lot. "I thought you said Thomas organized this reception just yesterday. It seems like half the town is here."

"You know what the Coconut Cove grapevine is like," I said. "News spreads fast. Now, you know what you need to do tonight, right?"

"Speak with Olivia," he said.

"I still can't believe you spent an hour with her yesterday and didn't manage to ask one question about the murder."

"Like I told you, we got so caught up in talking about video editing that it completely slipped my mind." He frowned. "I'm not really cut out to be an investigator."

I brushed his cheek with my fingers. "I'd have to agree. You seem to be missing the nosiness gene."

"I think you have enough of that for the both of us," he said after he kissed the back of my hand.

As we walked toward the building, I pointed out the topiary of Puss and Boots. "How do you think they managed to sculpt the plume on top of his hat?"

"Very carefully," Scooter said as he stopped to take some pictures. "Don't you think it would be fun to video Mrs. Moto in front of this?"

"Fun for you or fun for her?" I asked.

He put his arm around my shoulder. "Fun for the entire family. You could dress up with a hat and sword too."

"Not gonna happen. Come on, I'm starved. Jim is catering the reception. I hope he's serving those rosemary lamb kebabs."

As we walked in the door, the sounds of a string quartet filled the room along with the buzz of people chatting over drinks and appetizers. For someone who had only had an agreement in principle to buy back Coconut Creations, Thomas sure was pouring a lot of money into his grand reopening. I hoped that the widow didn't change her mind about the deal.

After grabbing a glass of champagne, I turned to Scooter. "Okay, let's split up. You go find Olivia and find out if she knew Gregor, if she saw anything that night, and if she knows how to use a knife. Whatever you do, don't let her change the subject. I'm going to go find Thomas."

As I wandered around the gallery for a while searching for our host, I spotted Penny looking at the watercolor miniatures of pink flowers. She seemed enchanted by them. I made a mental note to come back later in the week and pick one up for her birthday. When I couldn't find Thomas, one of the waitresses suggested that he might be in the garden behind the station.

I walked through the back door out onto the old train platform. The wooden benches had been cleverly turned into displays of ceramic outdoor statues, the kind you see dotted in people's gardens. I paused to examine a collection of cats dressed up like gnomes. It would probably be better if Scooter didn't see these, otherwise he'd be tempted to get Mrs. Moto a red-pointed hat.

I spotted a row of tall potted plants at the end of the platform. As I walked toward them, I heard two men talking. I paused to listen—only to see if one of them was Thomas, mind you. I wasn't eavesdropping. Or at least I wasn't eavesdropping until I heard the guys mention Gregor. Then I went into full investigation mode, hiding behind the planters and peeking through the leaves.

Jim was standing next to a fountain with his arms crossed. "You need to tell the police what happened."

"I can't," Thomas said. "They'll assume the worst."

"If you don't, someone innocent might get hurt," Jim said.

Thomas wrung his hands. "It won't come to that, I swear."

"I hope you can live with a guilty conscience," Jim said. He started to walk away when Thomas grabbed his arm. "You won't say anything, will you?"

Jim looked down at the ground for a few moments, then said something too quietly for me to hear. He pulled his arm away and started to walk back toward the building. I took that as my cue to scurry back inside before I was caught eavesdropping...I mean, investigating.

As I walked back through the gallery, I saw Scooter standing next to the buffet table. "Any luck with Olivia?" I asked.

He sighed. "Not really. I started to ask her about Gregor, but instead she suggested I try one of these." He pointed at something that resembled a pancake with smoked salmon and sour cream on top. "Try one. They're really good."

I popped one into my mouth. "Delicious. What are they called?"

"It sounded like she said 'bleen,'" he said as he handed me

a napkin. "I didn't really catch it."

Penny tapped me on the shoulder and pointed at the tray. "They're called 'blinis.' They're Russian, made out of buckwheat. Can you hand me one?"

"Olivia also told me about her favorite soup—borscht," Scooter said. "She seems to know a lot about Russian food."

"She does," Penny agreed. "She told me there was a Russian deli near her apartment in New York City that she would always go to." She grabbed another blini, then flitted off to speak with some friends.

"We really need to get that Russian note translated," I said to Scooter.

"Why don't you ask Olivia?" he suggested. "Seems like she might know some Russian."

"She's a suspect," I said. "Now that we know it's written in Russian, I'm not sure if it's connected to Chief Tyler or Gregor. If it's connected to Gregor, I don't want her to realize that we have it."

"But Sawyer saw it, and the two of them are friends. She may have already told her about it."

"That's a really good point," I said. "We'll make an investigator out of you yet." I pointed at the reception desk by the old train station ticket kiosk. "I see Sawyer over there. I'm going to talk to her and find out if she said anything to Olivia."

"Did you want to sign up for an art class?" Sawyer asked as I approached the desk.

"I'm not sure that would be a good idea. I can't even draw stick figures," I said.

She opened up a brochure and pointed at a picture of a group of smiling people holding up small paintings. "None of these people knew how to draw either before they took lessons from Thomas."

"I don't know," I said.

"Tell you what. Why don't you come to the presentation

tomorrow night? Some local artists are going to talk about different painting techniques and Thomas is going give an overview of the classes we offer. It'll be fun." She handed me a clipboard. "Here's the sign-up form."

"It says on here that Anabel and Victoria are going to be speaking."

"Uh-huh. Thomas spoke with both of them today and arranged it. Let's get you signed up." She opened one of the desk drawers and looked inside. "There's a pen around here somewhere." After pulling out a stack of papers from another drawer, she muttered, "Gregor left this place a mess. I can't find anything."

"I bet things were more organized when you worked here," I said.

"You bet they were," she replied as she hunted through another drawer.

"So, why did he fire you?" I asked.

Sawyer looked taken aback, then she leaned forward. "Between you and me, he was a bit of a creep. He made a pass at me. When I told him I wasn't interested, he told me that he no longer had need of my services."

"Was this when Victoria and he were dating?" I asked.

"Knowing his reputation, probably. But I'm not sure when the two of them started seeing each other. He certainly kept that under wraps."

As she placed a pack of highlighters on the desk, she knocked the stack of papers on the floor. I picked them up and sorted through them as I set them back down. Maybe there was some sort of clue in Gregor's old papers that would point to his murderer. Most of the papers were boring—letters from art dealers, bills from the electric company, and contracts with local artists.

"These look like receipts," I said, holding up a stack held together with a paper clip. "This one has those funny Cyrillic letters."

Sawyer grabbed it from my hand. "Yep. Looks Russian."

"Did you tell Olivia about the note I showed you last night, by any chance?" I asked.

"No. Why?"

"No reason." I handed her another receipt. "What about this one? Is it Russian too?"

"This one is in French," she said. "It looks like it's from Tahiti. Something to do with a cane, I think. My French is really rusty." She pulled out her phone. "Let's run it through a translator." She peered at the screen. "Yep. It's for a cane. Victoria's name and address is on top. It looks like she bought a walking cane and had it shipped to the States. Ooh. This is interesting. It says something about a knife hidden in the handle. Oh, my goodness. That was what killed Gregor, wasn't it?"

"You know about that?" I asked.

"Ben told me about it when the gang was at the Tipsy Pirate having drinks last night." She put her finger to her lips. "Actually, he told me to keep that to myself. You won't tell anyone, will you?"

"It's our little secret," I said before plucking the receipt from her hand. "Do you mind if I keep this?"

She shrugged. "Fine by me. This is all going to get tossed, anyway."

I took a moment to sip another glass of champagne and consider everything I had learned in that short period of time. Thomas was hiding something, possibly the fact that he had murdered Gregor. Victoria had purchased the murder weapon. Olivia had some knowledge of Russian, or at least of Russian food. And Sawyer had refused Gregor's advances, which was why he fired her. It was all a bit overwhelming.

Normally, I liked to bounce ideas off of Scooter, but he was engrossed in a conversation with Ned and Nancy. The older woman was pointing at a fire extinguisher. I could only imagine the scintillating discussion they were having about the regulations governing how many fire extinguishers you needed per square foot.

I wandered out to the train platform to get some fresh air and clear my head. The only problem was that the air wasn't very fresh. Victoria was pacing back and forth, a cigarette in hand. When she spotted me, she held up her pack. "Want one?"

"No, thanks," I said, stifling a cough. "I don't smoke."

"Smart. It's a nasty habit."

"Should you be smoking?" I asked. "I thought you were sick?"

"I probably shouldn't be. This is actually the first one I've had in months." She took a drag. "Stress, I guess."

"Are you stressed out because your fiancé died?" I asked.

"I'm actually happy he's dead now," she said, spitting out the words. "Turns out he was married."

"You didn't know?" I asked.

"Of course not," she said. "I wouldn't have dated a married man."

"You must regret buying him that expensive cane from Tahiti," I said.

"Don't be ridiculous," she said. "I didn't buy that for him."

I pulled the receipt out of my purse. "Are you sure about that?"

Her shoulders slumped. "Fine. I bought it for him."

"Why didn't you say anything before?" I asked.

"You know what the police are like. They would have jumped to conclusions."

"You mean they would have accused you of murder?"

"Exactly."

"But you just said that you're glad he's dead."

She threw her cigarette butt on the ground and stamped it out with her heel. "Sure, I'm glad he's dead, but I didn't kill him." As she turned to leave, she said over her shoulder. "The police already have the right woman under suspicion."

"You mean Anabel?" I asked incredulously.

She nodded, then walked back inside. Thoughts of what the chief had said about Gregor blackmailing Anabel kept popping into my mind. It couldn't be her, I told myself firmly. But why did a nagging voice in my head keep telling me not to be blinded by friendship?

* * *

When I woke up the next morning, my first thought was to check and see if Chief Dalton had called back. After Victoria admitted she had bought the cane for Gregor, I had left an urgent message for the chief. I was surprised that I hadn't heard anything back yet—this was the breakthrough in the case we had been hoping for.

I looked for my phone in all the usual places—by the bed, in my purse, and under the table where Mrs. Moto sometimes hid it. It was nowhere to be found. "Where did it go?" I asked the calico. She was too preoccupied batting around one of those plastic milk bottle rings to pay any attention to me.

I poured another cup of coffee and tried to reconstruct my movements from the previous night. Victoria had fessed up, then left the gallery in a hurry, claiming she didn't feel well. I had grabbed another one of those delicious kebabs and watched while Thomas ran after her. The kebab in hand, I had scooted out the door and followed them at a discreet distance. I tucked myself behind a large Snow White topiary and kept my eye on them while they had a very interesting argument.

"I can't keep covering for you," Thomas said, grabbing her elbow. "It's causing a strain on my relationship with Jim."

Victoria pulled her arm away. "I don't know what you're talking about."

"I saw you that night," he said. "I've done everything I could to try to protect you, but the lies are starting to catch up with me."

"Protect me? Hah! All you want to do is protect yourself." She waved her hands at the old railway station. "Looks like it's all worked out nicely for you. You have your gallery back." She pulled her keys out of her purse. "Just leave me alone. I don't want anything else to do with you. You didn't even tell me Gregor was married."

"I did too, but you were too stubborn to believe me. You wanted to believe that he had divorced his wife."

Victoria pointed her keys at him, started to say something, then stormed off without finishing her thought.

"We're family. I only want to help," he yelled after her. He looked deflated as he watched her pull out of the parking lot without a further word.

After their argument, I had paced around Snow White and the seven smaller dwarf topiaries while I thought about what I had heard. Victoria had definitely done it. Thomas had witnessed it and was covering it up. I remembered calling the chief again at that point and leaving another voice message. After hanging up, I had caught my heel in a grate. When I bent down to free it, I stumbled and fell.

Aha! That was it. I must have dropped my phone by the topiaries. I grabbed my purse and told Mrs. Moto to be a good girl while I was gone, then sped back to Coconut Creations.

When I got there, I noticed a few cars in the parking lot. It was too early for the gallery to be open. Most likely, some of the guests who had too much champagne had arranged alternative transportation home. After a brief search, I found my phone next to Pinocchio. While I was listening to my messages, I noticed that one of the vehicles looked like Victoria's.

What was she doing here? Was she meeting Thomas? While I called the chief back, I looked around to see if I could spot Thomas' car. Was that black sedan his?

"It's Mollie," I said after being put through to the chief's voicemail. "Call me back when you get this. I'm at the art gallery. Actually, scratch that. Get down here right away. And bring your handcuffs so you can arrest Victoria."

While I waited for backup, I heard a loud crash that sounded like it came from behind the old train station. I tiptoed around the topiaries until I reached the side of the building. My back flat against the brickwork, I inched my way down to the corner, then peeked my head around.

A large gray cat was crouched on one of the wooden benches running the length of the platform. He was staring down proudly at the shards of a broken ceramic statue. As he extended his paw to push another one on the feline gnomes to the ground, I waved my arms at him. He stared at me for a moment, then nonchalantly hopped down and batted at the shards. Before I could shoo him away, he streaked past me, leapt down onto the railway bed, and then sauntered across the abandoned tracks.

I watched as his fluffy gray tail disappeared behind some old weeds, then looked back at the platform. That's when I noticed a broken statue wasn't the only thing lying on the platform. There was also a gun. And next to the gun was a body. Victoria's body.

CHAPTER 13
MAGIC BEANS

I heard sirens blaring in the background. When I had left a voice message for Chief Dalton to meet me at the gallery, I didn't expect him to bring the cavalry. But seeing Victoria's lifeless body, it seemed like a good call on his part.

While I waited for the squad car to arrive, I had a closer look at the poor woman. I shook my head at the pack of cigarettes and lighter next to her. Turns out it wasn't smoking that ended up killing her. The silver lighter was interesting. It looked like an antique with some sort of engraving. As I bent down to have a closer look, I noticed a piece of folded paper tucked under the pack of cigarettes. I reached into my purse and took out a pencil. As I was using the pencil to pull the paper out from underneath the cigarettes, I heard someone walk up behind me.

"What exactly are you doing, Mrs. McGhie?"

I turned and saw Chief Dalton standing behind me. Ever since Anabel had been arrested, the chief had started to be more relaxed around me, even calling me by my first name. I wondered what had caused him to revert to his previous, formal, stiff demeanor. Then I saw the deputy next to him. Ah, it was probably for show. He didn't want his deputy to realize the two of us had become friends.

"I wanted to see what was on this paper, but I didn't want to contaminate the evidence, hence the pencil," I said. "But now that you're here, do you mind handing me a pair of gloves, Tiny?"

The burly man pursed his lips. "I'm going to have to ask you to step back, ma'am. Deputy, would you mind escorting Mrs. McGhie inside and have her wait there until I'm ready to take her statement?"

As I stood, he leaned toward me and hissed, "By the way, it's Chief Dalton, not Tiny." Then he stepped back. "I'll be with you shortly, ma'am."

I waited inside the art gallery on one of the overstuffed couches. Dirty dishes and empty champagne bottles were scattered on the various tables. Apparently, the cleaning crew hadn't been in yet. Around thirty minutes later, the chief walked in the room and sat next to me. He pulled a notebook out of his pocket and flipped it open.

"What time did you discover Miss Williams?" he asked without even as much as a glance at me.

"Right after I phoned you," I said.

He scratched down a note. "And when was that, ma'am?"

"Pull out your phone and check it," I snapped.

"Let's try another question. What were you doing at the art gallery?"

I clenched my fists. "I told you in my message. I came here to look for my phone."

"The same phone you allegedly called me from?"

"What the heck is wrong with you?" I asked. "Can you put your pen down and tell me what's going on. Who killed Victoria?"

He flipped over a page in his notebook. "Why do you think

it was murder?"

"Because we've been investigating a murder. Remember? Gregor's murder? Victoria was a suspect and now she's dead. The killer must have decided she was a danger to them and offed her."

"Do I need to remind you again, Mrs. McGhie, that you are not a member of the police force? Leave the investigating to the professionals."

"But, you were the one who asked me to help clear Anabel's name!" I took a few deep breaths, trying to recall Thomas' relaxation exercise. I was worried that I was going to start developing high blood pressure myself given the chief's attitude toward me. As I exhaled, I looked at the burly man. "I don't get what's come over you, I really don't. I'd think you'd want to get to the bottom of Victoria's murder before someone tries to pin this one on Anabel as well."

Chief Dalton put his notebook down on the couch and walked over to where his deputy was standing by the door. They had a quiet discussion, then the deputy handed him a plastic evidence bag and went outside.

"It wasn't murder," the chief said as he handed the bag to me. "It was suicide. She left a note."

I gasped as I read what Victoria had written:

Dear Thomas - You were right. I can't allow someone else to be falsely accused for what I did. I was the one who killed Gregor. I was angry about the affairs he was having with other women while we were seeing each other. When he proposed to me at Warlock's Manor, I believed that he had changed.

During the night, I woke up with a headache and went into the bathroom to get a painkiller. Gregor had left his phone on the sink. I picked it up and saw that he had a text message. I know I shouldn't have, but I read it and that's when I discovered he was married. It was from his wife asking when he was coming home. I started sobbing.

Gregor heard me and came into the bathroom. He told me

to be quiet otherwise I would wake everyone up. He talked me into going outside to discuss things. As we walked down the dock, he promised me that he was getting a divorce, but I knew he was lying. In my anger I pushed him and he dropped his cane. As I grabbed it, I remembered how I had given it him it as a gift. I don't know what came over me, but I was so angry that I...well, you know what happened. I killed him.

I can't live with the pain anymore—the pain of knowing what I did and the pain of knowing that Gregor never loved me. Soon, I won't have to live with this pain anymore.

I handed the letter back to the chief. "Wow," was all I could think to say.

"As you can see, there's no need for an investigation. This is cut and dry," the chief said stiffly. Then he added in a gentler voice, "I did appreciate your help and how you went to bat for Anabel, but we can put this to bed now. Things are back to normal."

He picked up his notebook and got up from the couch. "Oh, no," he muttered. "What's he doing here?"

I twisted my body to see what was going on. Chief Tyler was standing in the entryway. He was wearing a similar outfit to when I had seen him on Destiny Key—olive green shorts and a lighter green shirt—except this time, he was sporting a shiny badge and a police belt.

"Dalton," he said as he chewed on a toothpick.

"Tyler," was the Coconut Cove chief of police's terse response.

"I understand you've had some excitement here," Chief Tyler said.

"Don't you have enough excitement on Destiny Key?"

"Nah. Nothing out of the ordinary ever happens there," the scrawny man said. "That's on account of the fact that I run a tight ship there."

"What are you doing here, Tyler?"

"Well, me and the missus came into town for a few days.

She wanted to have a fancy meal at Chez Poisson and stay at that boutique hotel. I'm not crazy about this town of yours, but it's what she wanted, so..." He shrugged as his voice trailed off.

I leaned over the back of the couch. "I think what he meant is what are you doing here, at the art gallery?"

"I'll ask the questions here, Mrs. McGhie," Chief Dalton said. When the other chief smirked, he added, "What are you doing at the gallery, Tyler?"

"I heard you've got the person who killed Gregor Smirnov. Thought I would come check things out. His murder did happen in my jurisdiction."

"It looks like you can close that case now. Victoria Williams murdered him, then killed herself. If you head out back, my deputy can show you the body and fill you in." Chief Dalton's eyes bored into his rival's back as he watched him go through the door. Then he turned to me. "Why don't you head home, Mollie? Things could get ugly here, and I don't want you mixed up in it."

As I walked back to my car, I felt my stomach churning. Something was bugging me about this situation and it wasn't just Chief Dalton's hot and cold manner toward me. Victoria's suicide seemed too convenient, too easy of an answer. As I looked at the topiary of Jack and the Beanstalk, I chided myself for trying to make things more complicated than they were. There weren't any 'magic beans' at work here, just a simple murder-suicide as Chief Dalton had said. Be happy that Anabel was free from suspicion and let the matter drop, I told myself.

* * *

Later that night, I went back to the gallery for the art presentation. I was surprised it was still taking place, but apparently clearing the scene of a suicide takes a lot less time than that of a murder. When I walked inside, Thomas was hanging a painting on the far wall. After he positioned it, he stepped back and sighed loudly.

"Is that one of Victoria's?" I asked, looking at the seascape.

"Yes. It's one of the few that wasn't damaged." He pressed his fingertips underneath his eyes as if holding back tears.

"The two of you were close, weren't you?" I asked.

"We were practically raised together," he said. "She was my cousin on my mother's side."

I thought back to the previous night in the parking lot when Thomas had said something to her about being family. I had assumed he meant a metaphorical family, the community of artists.

"Is that why she addressed her suicide note to you?"

He raised his eyebrows. "You saw it?"

"Yes. Chief Dalton showed it to me. You do know that I was the one who found her, don't you?"

He fiddled with one of his cufflinks. "Sorry, the chief told me that. With everything that happened, it slipped my mind."

"Why don't you cancel tonight's event?" I asked. "Everyone would understand. You lost a member of your family."

He straightened his shoulders. "No, she would have wanted me to carry on. Getting more people interested in art was important to her."

"It sounds like a nice tribute to her."

He nodded.

"Do you mind if I ask you something? In her note, Victoria said something about you being right about not keeping things a secret. Did you know that she had killed Gregor?"

Thomas chewed his lip for a moment. "I suppose it doesn't matter now..." He choked back a sob. "Now that she's passed. I saw her that night. I had gone downstairs to check on the generator. I looked out the bay window and saw her standing on the dock. The storm had passed, and the skies were clear.

She was illuminated by the moonlight. Her white nightgown glowed like that of an angel."

"Was Gregor there?" I asked.

"No, not then. I guess it was right after she..." His voice trailed off as he pressed his fingers to his face again.

I put my hand on his arm. "It's okay. You don't have to talk about it."

"Thanks," he said. "Somehow I feel responsible. If only I had seen her earlier and spoken with her, maybe I could have prevented it."

"Don't beat yourself up. You couldn't have known. She seemed happy when she went to bed that night."

"That's what Jim keeps telling me."

"What was she like when she came back in the house?"

"I didn't see her until the next day. I checked the generator, then went back to bed." He looked at the clock above the ticket kiosk. "I have time to hang one more of these before the session starts. Why don't you head into the back room and mingle? There's some coffee and cookies as well. Help yourself."

I should have offered to assist Thomas with the painting, but when someone mentions cookies, I tend to forget my manners. Plus, it seemed like he wanted some time to himself.

While I was picking up a lemon bar, Anabel rushed over and gave me a hug. "I can't believe you found Victoria like that," she said. "How awful."

"You must be relieved that Chief Tyler no longer has a case against you," I said.

"I am," she admitted. "But that isn't the way I wanted it to happen. That poor woman is dead."

"Tiny must be happy too," I said.

"Oh, he is," she said. "He's glad he can focus on his job again."

I smirked. "You mean handing out parking tickets?"

"Are you talking about Chief Dalton?" Ben asked as he

reached around me to grab a chocolate chip cookie. "He's set up a new speed trap near Alligator Chuck's BBQ Joint. I almost got nailed today."

"What a surprise to see you here," Anabel said to Ben. "I didn't know you were interested in art."

"He's not," I said. "He's interested in Sawyer. I saw you chatting her up when I walked in here."

"Guilty," Ben said as he wiped crumbs off his shirt. "I wanted to ask her out, but Olivia wouldn't take the hint. She kept standing there talking about the best way to crack open a coconut."

"She should move to Coconut Cove," I said. "People are obsessed with coconuts here."

Ben rolled his eyes. "She'd fit right in."

"What method does she use?" Anabel asked.

"She uses a machete. You whack the pointier end of the coconut with it until you get to the meat. She's got a video of her demonstrating the process in Tahiti if you want to check it out."

"Can everyone take their seats and we'll get started," Thomas said as he adjusted his zebra-striped bow tie. He kicked off his presentation by showing us works painted in different styles and asked us which ones we preferred. Melvin favored Renaissance art, Ben liked the abstracts, and I was drawn to Warhol's pop art, especially his Marilyn Monroe series.

But my favorite part of the session was when he showed us paintings done by animals including whales, chimpanzees, elephants, and even bunny rabbits. The world better watch out, I thought. Once Scooter found out about this, he was going to get Mrs. Moto a set of paints and canvases and let her loose on camera.

After an hour, Thomas suggested we all take a coffee break. When I told Ben and Olivia about turning Mrs. Moto into an artist, Ben asked us if we knew what the unluckiest kind of cat was to have. We groaned when he told us it was a catastrophe.

"That was such a bad dad joke," I said.

"I better hurry up and get married and have kids so I can embarrass them," he said.

"I wish my father had limited himself to just telling bad dad jokes," Olivia said. "That wouldn't be half as embarrassing as all the other stuff he did."

"Like what?" Ben asked.

"He's one of those guys that always talks without thinking first. There was this time that one of my friends spent the night at my house." She took a sip of coffee, then continued. "You know how when you have a really bad cold, you snore? It's not your fault. You can't help it. Well, my friend was all stuffed up and, let's just say, I'm surprised she could sleep through her own snoring."

"Well, the next morning over breakfast, my father joked that he couldn't sleep all night because there was an elephant sleeping in the next room. Then he made these trumpeting sounds. He thought he was being funny, but he wasn't. The poor girl was mortified. You should have heard my mother tear into him. 'Misha, keep it up and you'll be the one sleeping on the couch tonight.'"

"Colds are the worst," Ben said. "Sawyer sounds like she's coming down with one. I heard her sniffling earlier."

"She said something about her allergies acting up," Olivia said. "They were bugging her on Destiny Key as well." She looked over at Sawyer, who was chatting with Anabel at the front of the room. "Don't say anything but Sawyer was snoring like a freight train when we were there. I even moved to the couch to get some shut-eye." She grabbed a cookie, then scooted off to check with Thomas about the next part of the presentation.

"You better not say anything to Sawyer about her snoring," I said to Ben as we walked back to our seats. "She'd be horrified if she knew Olivia told you about that."

"Of course, I wouldn't," he said. "I'm not a blabbermouth."

"Really? How come Sawyer knew that the knife that killed Gregor was part of his cane?"

Ben hemmed and hawed, before suggesting that we sit down.

After everyone was back in their places, Thomas said, "All right, I'm going to hand things over to local artist, Anabel Dalton. She's best known for her fanciful oil paintings of magical creatures. You may have seen some of her work on display at the Sailor's Corner Cafe. She also exhibits at arts and craft fairs around the state. I'm delighted to announce that she's agreed to find time in her busy schedule to be one of our art instructors."

"How many of you are right-handed?" Anabel asked as she walked up to the front of the room. The majority of the people raised their hands, including me. "And the left-handers?" Ben and another young guy high-fived each other in solidarity as fellow southpaws. "Is anyone ambidextrous?" Sawyer scanned the room. "No one? That doesn't surprise me. Only one percent of the population can use both their left and right hands equally well. For the rest of us, when we try to do something with our non-dominant hand, it's quite challenging."

"I broke my left wrist when I was a kid. It was in a cast for a month," Ben said. "My teacher had to give me extra time on my English test because it took me so long to write with my right hand."

Sawyer chuckled. "I remember that. You tried to blame your failing grade on the fact that your handwriting was illegible."

"But that was the reason why," Ben protested.

"You don't think it had to do with the fact that you didn't read the book?" Sawyer asked.

The room burst out laughing. Ben wagged his finger at her.

"I'll get you back later, Miss Smarty Pants."

Anabel held up her hands for silence. "Tell you what, why don't we do an exercise where we can all experience what Ben went through?" She passed out two pieces of sketching paper and a pencil to everyone. "On the first piece of paper, I want you to use your dominant hand. Write your name and today's date at the top, then draw a simple picture of a tree, clouds, and the sun. You have five minutes."

Once everyone had finished, she pointed at Melvin. "Do you mind holding up your drawing?"

"It's not very good," he said as he reluctantly got to his feet.

"I think you're being hard on yourself," Anabel said, patting him on the back. "I like the shading around the clouds. Very creative. Let's talk about how it felt to do this exercise. What was it like writing your name and the date?"

Melvin shrugged. "Fine. Normal."

"Did you have to think about it?" Anabel asked.

"No. It's something I do every day," he said.

"So it was a normal, everyday activity? Nothing out of the ordinary?"

Melvin nodded.

"You can go ahead and have a seat. Okay, let's do the same thing, but this time with your non-dominant hand." She looked at her phone. "Five minutes starting now."

A couple of girls giggled as they compared their pictures. An older man broke his pencil as he awkwardly gripped it in his left hand while attempting to write his name. I almost crumpled up my paper after the sun I was trying to draw ended up more square-shaped than circular.

"Time," Anabel said. "Mollie, how about if you be our volunteer this time?"

"This is so embarrassing," I said as I held up my paper.

"You shouldn't be embarrassed, you should be proud that you tried to do something you're not used to doing. I think your tree looks great."

"That's supposed to be a cloud," I said.

"A cloud? Oh, yes, I see it now," she said, peering at my drawing. "Now, how did you feel during that exercise?"

"It was frustrating," I said. "I felt anxious that I wouldn't get it done in time."

"Those are all perfectly natural reactions," Anabel said. "But the important thing to remember is that all of you were able to do this exercise with your non-dominant hand. Sure, it might have felt awkward, frustrating, and difficult but you all did it. You created something despite the limitations I placed on you."

Thomas walked up to the front of the room. "Using your non-dominant hand is a great way to get in touch with the creative side of your brain. One of the reasons I asked Anabel to lead this exercise is to show you the types of activities you'll do in our introductory art class. Not only will you have fun and a lot of laughs, you'll also get to explore different techniques." He held up a clipboard. "I have a sign-up sheet which I'll leave up front. Anabel, Sawyer, and I will also be happy to answer any questions you have."

"Are you going to sign up?" Ben asked.

"I think so," I said. "How about you?"

"Sure thing. Sawyer is one of the teachers." He smiled, pointing at my paper. "Maybe by the end of the course, your clouds won't look like trees."

As I looked again at the cloud I had tried to draw with my left hand, it hit me. There was no way Victoria could have committed suicide. She had been murdered.

CHAPTER 14
EXTRA KETCHUP

"Whoa, whoa. Slow down," Scooter said. "Start again at the beginning. Why do you think Victoria was murdered?"

After the presentation was over I had rushed to my car without saying goodbye to anyone. Once inside, I made sure the doors were locked, then I called my husband. "It's because of her hand. Remember how she was wearing a wrist brace? When we first met her at our splash party, she mentioned that she had carpal tendonitis. She was struggling to hold a paintbrush with her right hand. It got worse at the artists' retreat."

"That's right," Scooter said. "When we were at Warlock's Manor, she tried to pour some brandy into her glass and almost dropped the bottle. Thomas had to grab it from her."

"She couldn't grip anything with that hand. How in the world would she have managed to hold a gun and shoot herself with it?"

"Could she have done it with her left hand?" he asked.

"I doubt it. She had problems with that one, as well. Not as bad as her right, but still."

"Where are you now?" Scooter asked.

"At the gallery."

"I want you to get back here—"

"Hang on a sec," I said, peering through the windshield. "Sawyer, Olivia, and Thomas are all standing at the front of the building talking about something. It's scary to think one of them killed Gregor and Victoria."

"Mollie, get back to the boat now," Scooter said frantically. "Do not talk to them. Once you're back, we'll call Chief Dalton and have him take it from here."

"No way," I said. "You should have seen the way he treated me earlier. All 'Mrs. McGhie this' and 'Mrs. McGhie that.' He wants to believe that Victoria did it. I need proof that she didn't commit suicide before he'll take me seriously."

Scooter sighed. "We'll talk about it when you get back."

"Okay," I said.

Before I could hang up, he added, "And no stops on the way back."

"Not even for a cheeseburger and fries?"

After a pause, he said. "Okay. But only if you go through the drive-through. And can you get extra ketchup this time?"

* * *

The next morning, Scooter decided to take Mrs. Moto to the beach for a photo shoot. Before he left, he made me promise not to do anything foolish. When I asked him what he meant by 'foolish,' he said questioning of, eavesdropping on, or following Thomas, Olivia, and Sawyer. The previous night, he had phoned Chief Dalton and explained my theory about Victoria's death. The chief thanked him and said he'd look into it. Scooter took him at his word. I, on the other hand, didn't believe him. Chief Dalton was far more interested in how much revenue his new speed trap could generate than reopening Victoria's case.

When Scooter and Mrs. Moto left, he expanded on his definition of 'foolish,' telling me that I shouldn't gorge myself on the bag of mini Snickers bars, reminding me that the last time I had done that, I had complained about having a tummy ache.

I nodded, waved goodbye, stretched out on the settee, and unwrapped a chocolate bar. What's great about Snickers bars is that they have peanuts in them. Peanuts are basically mini protein pellets and protein is good for you. Protein builds muscle. And you need muscles when you live on a boat. Sailing can be hard work.

While I continued to build muscle mass, I leafed through a marine equipment catalog, pausing to look at the pictures of dinghies. There was no way we could afford to buy a new one. We were going to have to retrieve the one we had left at Warlock's Manor. I decided to put Operation Destiny Key into action. I would go to the island, check on our dinghy, and figure out how to get it back. Scooter would be pleased with how I was going to spend the day—it wasn't in the least possible way foolish. Chief Tyler was still celebrating his anniversary on the mainland so I wouldn't run into him. And there wouldn't be any temptation to question, eavesdrop on, or follow Olivia, Sawyer, or Thomas, as they wouldn't be on the island either.

I congratulated myself. It was a highly sensible plan. Then I realized that there was one tiny problem. I had no way to get to the island. The ferry service didn't operate on Saturdays. I pondered this while I unwrapped another chocolate bar. Then inspiration struck—Melvin had a boat, and he had mentioned the other day that anytime I wanted to go for a ride to call him.

So I did. After arranging to meet him at the public dock, I called Thomas. Now, before you start telling me that was 'foolish,' let me explain. I didn't question him about the murders. And Gregor and Victoria's names never came up. It couldn't be considered eavesdropping because we were having a conversation. You can't eavesdrop on yourself. And I wasn't following him. I was on board *Marjorie Jane,* lying down and rubbing my stomach because for some reason it felt a bit sore.

When I explained to Thomas that I wanted to check on our dingy, he told me that the owner of Warlock's Manor, Michael, wouldn't mind and that we should feel free to borrow the golf cart he left in town to drive to the house. Then he told me that he was holding a going-away party for Olivia at the Tipsy Pirate the next day and that we should come. I started to tell him that Scooter might think it was a foolish idea, then stopped myself and told Thomas that I'd check our calendar and get back to him.

* * *

The ride to Destiny Key on Melvin's boat was fun. While I enjoy the slower pace and tranquility of sailing, there's something to be said for zipping along in a powerboat. When we got to the island's public dock, we tied up on the rickety pier alongside some fishing boats. After walking past the ferry terminal, we followed a gravel road that wound through a desolate wooded area. Crows circled above us, cawing loudly, and the turkey vultures flapped their wings and screeched as we neared them.

"This is spooky," I said.

"Did Thomas say how far it was to the town?" Melvin asked. "I don't know why they can't leave the golf carts by the ferry dock."

"Less than ten minutes." I said "But it seems like we've been walking longer than that."

"Hopefully, it's around this bend," Melvin said, eyeing up the dark storm clouds forming overhead. "Looks like we might be getting some weather."

As large drops of rain started to fall, we picked up the pace. "Here we are," I said when we reached the end of the road. Tudor-style buildings were clustered around a town square. A large fountain stood in the middle of the square. At the center of the fountain was a statue of a pirate encircled by dolphins. "I think that's Coconut Carl," I said.

"We can check it out later. I see a cafe," Melvin said. "Let's get a coffee while we wait for the rain to stop. Then we can grab the golf cart and head to Warlock's Manor."

After deciding what we wanted—a large Americano for Melvin and a snickerdoodle macchiato for me—I tried to get the barista's attention. He was standing with his back to us, arranging pastries on a tray. I cleared my throat loudly then said "excuse me" a number of times, before ringing the bell on the counter. No response.

"Maybe he's deaf," Melvin suggested.

The barista turned and briefly made eye contact. Then he started folding cloth napkins and placing them in a basket, studiously ignoring us. I reached out and tapped him on the arm. "Can we order, please?"

He pulled his arm back and brushed his sleeve as though there was a piece of lint on it that he wanted to remove.

"I don't think we're getting anywhere," Melvin said. "Maybe we should go."

A man who bore a striking resemblance to Colonel Sanders approached the counter. I expected him to pull a piece of fried chicken out of the pocket of his white suit at any moment and offer it to us. I was kind of disappointed when he didn't.

"Tanner, can't you see that these fine people would like to be served?" the man asked.

The barista shrugged. "Don't recognize them."

"Guess he isn't deaf," Melvin whispered to me.

I put my hands on my hips. "Let me see if I've got this

right, Tanner. You need to recognize a customer before you serve them?"

"That's the way it works," Tanner said. "Need to be introduced properly first."

The Colonel Sanders lookalike chuckled. "What's your name, ma'am?"

"Mollie McGhie," I said.

He took my hand in his and gently shook it. "I'm Silas de Vries. It's a pleasure to make your acquaintance."

After he released my hand, I held it to my nose. Was that the Colonel's secret blend of herbs and spices that I smelled?

My stomach growled while Silas introduced himself to Melvin. Then the colonel turned to the barista. "Tanner, allow me to introduce you to Mollie and Melvin. Melvin, Mollie, this is Tanner."

Tanner nodded. "What can I get you folks?" he asked, then busied himself preparing our coffee drinks.

"Sorry about that. We don't get many strangers on Destiny Key," Silas explained.

"There was a bunch of them at Warlock's Manor last weekend," Tanner said while pouring frothy steamed milk over espresso.

"Ah, yes," Silas said. "I heard about that. Gregor Smirnov borrowed my golf cart to meet someone there."

"You knew Gregor?" I asked.

"Yes. I'm an art collector," he said. "Gregor helped add things to my collection."

"Ah, so you're the client he was visiting on the island," I said. "You must have been shocked when you found out he was murdered."

"Murder? I think you're mistaken," Silas said. "It was an accidental death. The poor man drowned."

Tanner handed Melvin his Americano. "My uncle said it turned out to be murder. The man's mistress did it."

"Is that right?" Silas grinned. "I'm not surprised. Gregor

always had a way with the ladies. The only problem is that there was usually more than one lady at time. I always told him that a jealous woman would be the death of him."

"He was also married," I said.

"Yes. His wife is a lovely woman. I dined with her and Gregor several times in New York City. She always made the most delicious borscht." He smacked his fingers to his lips, then turned to Tanner. "Did your uncle say which of Gregor's mistresses killed him?"

"A woman named Victoria," the barista said. He punched some keys on an old-fashioned cash register. "That will be twenty dollars."

"Twenty dollars for two coffees?" Melvin asked, raising his eyebrows.

Tanner was unapologetic. "This is an island. We have to import everything. It adds to the cost."

As I reached into my purse to pull out my wallet, a Coconut Creations brochure fell out. Silas picked it up, then pointed at a picture of an oil painting on the front. "I recognize this. It's one of the few originals painted by Mikhail Petrov." He leaned in and whispered, "Almost everything else he did was a forgery. Gregor used to help him pass them off as originals. He made a fortune in the process."

"Weren't you worried Gregor would sell you a forgery?" I asked.

"I could never be fooled by a fake," he said haughtily. Then he looked sideways at me. "It was quite the scandal when Mikhail and his wife were arrested. They were waiting to board a flight to Paris when the police swooped in. Rumor has it that someone ratted them out. They were so close to making their escape. They had forged passports and disguises." Silas smiled. "I saw pictures of them in the papers. Anastasia looked good as a brunette. She should have worn wigs more often."

"I think I remember that," Melvin said. "It happened

around ten years ago, right?"

Silas nodded. "Their poor daughter, Oksana, was distraught. She had just turned eighteen at the time. She changed her name after that and tried to build a new life for herself."

"Children should never be blamed for the sins of the parents," Melvin said.

"That's true, but unfortunately they often are," I said as I pulled my debit card out of my wallet.

Silas pushed my hand away. "There's no need for that. It's my treat. Tanner, add their bill to my tab."

Tanner opened a ledger and made a notation with a fountain pen, then asked me, "Why exactly are you on Destiny Key?"

"We're here to check on my dinghy. We left it at Warlock's Manor last weekend. Michael, the owner, gave us permission to visit the house."

"Your cousin always was an odd bird," Silas said to Tanner.

"Michael is your cousin?" I asked

"Second cousin, twice removed," Tanner said.

"Are you by any chance also related to Chief Tyler?" I asked.

"Yep."

"Everyone on Destiny Key is related to one another somehow," Silas explained. "Well, almost everyone. Occasionally, someone marries a mainlander."

I looked behind me as the door to the cafe opened, then I whispered to Melvin, "We should probably get going." I quickly thanked Silas for the coffee, then put my sunglasses on and pulled my hat down on my head before rushing outside.

"Why are you in such a hurry all of a sudden?" Melvin asked.

"Look behind you casually," I said. "See those two goons? They work for Chief Tyler. They aren't exactly the type of guys you want to run into."

* * *

As we drove down the road in our borrowed golf cart, I kept looking over my shoulder to make sure we weren't being followed.

"Are you sure going to Warlock's Manor is a good idea?" Melvin asked.

"Of course it is." I slowed down as we approached a giant puddle, skirting around it to avoid getting splashed.

"You don't sound very convincing," he said. "Maybe we should head back to Coconut Cove."

"It'll be fine," I said. "We have permission from the owner of the house to be here and this is a public road. We have as much right to be on it as anyone."

"But what about those two guys at the cafe?" Melvin asked. "Were they the ones you were telling me about who threatened you on the public beach the night Anabel was arrested?"

"Uh-huh."

"They carry guns, right?"

I tapped the side of my head. "Yeah, but we've got smarts."

"The smart thing to do would be to turn around," Melvin said.

"Look, I can see the house from here. We'll just check on the dinghy and go. It won't take long." As I pulled up in front of Warlock's Manor, I added, "And just to show you how much I appreciate your help, dinner's on me at Alligator Chuck's BBQ Joint next weekend. You know how much you love their ribs."

Melvin's eyes lit up. "Chuck should bottle his mesquite sauce. I'd buy it by the gallon." Then he patted his stomach. "Actually, maybe it's better that he doesn't sell it. My doctor told me I need to watch what I eat and exercise more."

"How about if we get a little exercise in and find the dinghy?" I asked.

As we walked down the beach, I pointed out where I had discovered Gregor's body.

"Wait a minute," I said. "I don't see *TARDIS*."

"*TARDIS*?" Melvin asked.

"That's what I named our dinghy." I grimaced. "Unlike with our sailboat, which already came with a name I would have never chosen—*Marjorie Jane*—I had free rein to name our dinghy, so I picked something cute."

"But what does *TARDIS* mean?"

"I take it you're not a sci-fi fan"

"Can't say that I am."

"Have you heard of *Doctor Who*?"

Melvin scratched his head. "Is that the new dentist?"

"No, it's a great television show about this Time Lord who travels around in a spaceship that looks like an old British telephone booth. He calls it a TARDIS, which stands for Time and Relative Dimension in Space. Basically, the inside is bigger than the outside. I'm amazed at how much we can fit in our dinghy. It's bigger than it looks." I shuddered as I thought of Gregor's body lying inside our *TARDIS*.

"Well, they can go pretty fast if you have a decent-sized engine, but probably not fast enough to travel through space," Melvin said.

"Probably not," I agreed. "But where did our *TARDIS* go? We left it right on the other side of the dock. I bet Chief Tyler and his goons stole it."

"Maybe they just moved it," Melvin suggested. He looked down at the sandy beach. "See these marks? They could be from a dinghy being dragged. Probably recently, since they haven't been washed away by rain."

We followed the trail to the shed. "Here it is," I said when I opened the door. "Or at least part of it. The outboard motor is missing."

"They probably took it off to make it easier to get the dinghy in here," Melvin said. "Do you see it propped up anywhere?"

I looked around the shed. It looked the same as the last time I had been in there—gardening supplies, tools, paint cans, cardboard boxes, and lots of other clutter scattered about. The only new addition was my dinghy crowding the center of the floor. The motor wasn't anywhere in sight.

"Hang on," I said. "Let me check behind these shelves." As I hopped over the dinghy to get to the other side of the shed, I felt something land in my hair. I frantically shook my head. A spider crawled onto my shoulder, causing me to yelp.

Melvin poked his head through the door. "Are you okay?"

"I'm fine," I said in a shaky voice as I brushed the spider off me. When it landed on my foot, I jerked my leg back, causing me to lose my balance and crash into the shelving unit. "Just a little misunderstanding between me and a spider," I said as I landed on the ground.

I grabbed a trowel to protect myself and Melvin said, "Don't kill it. Spiders are good luck."

"I'm not going to kill it. I just want to shoo it away." When I spotted my multi-legged foe, I said, "Aha, there you are!" while waving the trowel in its direction. But instead of scaring the spider off, I knocked a sack off the shelf. I looked down in dismay at the potting soil that spilled out of it and into the dinghy.

At least I thought it was potting soil. At first glance it looked like normal soil, but as I peered more closely, I noticed purple glitter mixed in. Strange. Maybe it was some sort of fertilizer. I scooped it back in the bag with the trowel, then set it back on the shelf. That's when I decided that Melvin was right after all—spiders were good luck.

I stood and brushed my shorts off, then joined Melvin outside. I held up a torn piece of paper triumphantly. "Look what I found. Right next to the potting soil. I would have never have found it if it hadn't been for that spider."

"What is it?" he asked.

"It looks like the other half of a note I found the day I discovered Gregor's body." I held it up. "See these letters? They're Russian. Now all I need to do is put the two halves together and translate it."

Melvin cocked his head to one side. "Why do you want to do that?"

"Don't you get it? I think it might have something to do with the murder. Maybe it's a clue that will help me figure out who killed Gregor and Victoria.

"But Victoria killed Gregor, then killed herself," he said.

"Not exactly."

After I explained to Melvin that Victoria's suicide had been faked, he gripped my arm. "Now we really need to get out of here," he said. "I thought the murder investigation was over and done with."

I tucked the note in my pocket, then held up my dirt-covered hands. "Okay, just let me clean up first, then we can go."

Melvin waited on the porch swing while I washed my hands in the kitchen sink. Before going back outside to join him, I stuck my head in the drawing room. I remembered that Thomas had said that he had been in the drawing room the night Gregor was killed. When he looked out the window, he had seen Victoria standing on the dock. Had he really seen his cousin standing there or had it been someone else?

Realizing that there was no way of knowing who Thomas had seen, I spun around to have another look at the room. I could picture that night clearly in my mind—Victoria and Anabel sitting on one couch by the fireplace and Olivia and Sawyer on the other. As the events surrounding Gregor's murder went through my mind, I noticed a saucer on the floor.

It was probably the one Mrs. Moto had been drinking milk

from while the rest of us were having brandy. I should have cleaned it up that night rather than leaving it lying there. When I bent down to grab it, I saw ashes in the fireplace grate. We hadn't had a fire the night we were there. And who in their right mind would light a fire in Florida in July, anyway? It's way too hot and humid here for that.

Maybe Thomas had lit one when he was here on his own, stubbornly waiting to catch the ferry rather than go back with the rest of us on the regatta boats. There would have been plenty of fallen tree branches to burn. I shrugged. I guess it didn't really matter why Thomas had made a fire. To each his own.

As I picked up the saucer, I realized that the fact that Thomas had started a fire actually was important. Sitting at the edge of the hearth was a piece of wood that hadn't been completely burned. What was interesting about this particular piece was that it had intricate carvings on it. Last I checked, trees in Florida didn't have intricate carvings on them. The only thing I knew that looked like that was Gregor's cane.

I sat back down on the floor. We had found the top part of the cane with the knife attached to it by Gregor's body, but we had never found the bottom half. Apparently Thomas had. But where and when? And why had he tried to burn the evidence?

CHAPTER 15
ROAD HOGS

The next morning, I went for a walk at a nearby nature reserve to clear my head. When Melvin and I returned to Coconut Cove the previous afternoon, Chief Dalton met us at the dock and took custody of the two additional pieces of evidence I had recovered—the piece of wood from Gregor's cane and the other half of the note. He assured me that he was keeping an open mind about Victoria's death. I assured him that I was keeping an open mind as well, except mine wasn't about whether or not Victoria had committed suicide. I knew she had been murdered. Instead, mine was about who had done it.

And that's why I found myself wandering along a boardwalk that wound through the saltwater marsh near Sunshine Bay. I needed some peace and quiet to ponder my list of suspects.

After crossing over a bridge and waving at some kayakers, I sat on a park bench and pulled out my phone. I had tried to translate the Russian note using an app, but it still seemed like it was written in code. It mentioned a painting called "The Dishonor of Mikhail and Anastasia" and that the price to acquire it was one hundred thousand dollars. It then said that the deal would be finalized on Destiny Key. Otherwise, it would be sold at auction.

The note clearly had something to do with Gregor—he bought and sold artwork, and he spoke Russian. It most likely had something to do with his meeting with his client, Silas de Vries, the Colonel Sanders lookalike who Melvin and I had encountered at the cafe on the island. Gregor had probably dropped it in the shed, but why had he been in there in the first place?

I sighed and tucked my phone in my pocket. I still hadn't figured out who the killer was. The only thing I had learned was that art was expensive. Can you imagine having a hundred thousand dollars to spend on a painting?

As I was heading back to the parking lot, a man on a bike sped toward me from the opposite direction. He was in the middle of the path, oblivious to the fact that it was meant to be shared by pedestrians and cyclists. As he approached me, I had to press against the railing to keep from being run over. "Hey, watch where you're going, buddy," I yelled as he zipped around a bend in the path.

"Moron," I muttered as I continued walking. While I was pulling out my phone to check the time, I heard a rattling noise behind me. I spun around and saw the bike barreling straight at me. The cyclist reached behind his back, pulled out a gun from the waistband of his shorts, and pointed it straight at me. When an evil grin spread across his face, I recognized him. Had Chief Tyler had sent one of his goons after me?

* * *

"Are you all right, miss?" I heard a voice ask.

I opened my eyes and saw a man kneeling over me. A

woman was standing behind him, her hands clutching the handle of a double stroller.

"That lunatic could have knocked the twins over," she said. "I can't believe they let bikes in here."

"Did you see him?" I asked as the man helped me up.

He pointed at a fork in the path. "We had just come from there when we saw him knock you down. I rushed over to make sure you were okay."

"It was lucky you came along when you did," I said, thinking about how close I had come to getting shot.

"No kidding," he said. "There aren't many people out here today. What if you had been seriously hurt? You could have been lying here for hours all alone."

"How do you feel?" the woman asked.

I rubbed the back of my neck. It felt stiff, but that seemed to be the extent of my injuries. "I think I'm fine. Maybe a bruise or two from falling against the railing."

The woman handed one of the twins a stuffed animal, then picked up the other one and fussed over him. "You're lucky you didn't fall into the water. There's crocodiles in there."

I wanted to tell her that crocodiles were the least of my worries. Instead, I asked them if they wouldn't mind walking me back to my car. After they waved goodbye, I called Chief Dalton.

"One of Tyler's henchmen tried to kill me," I said, then explained how a young family had inadvertently saved my life. While the goon might have been happy to shoot me if I had been on my own, dealing with witnesses was more problematic and it seemed he had chickened out.

"What you found at Warlock's Manor must be really incriminating," the chief said. "Otherwise, Tyler wouldn't be trying to eliminate you."

"But I didn't find anything that had to do with him," I said.

"Of course you did. That note in Russian or that piece of the cane must tie Tyler to the murders of Mr. Smirnov and

Miss Williams. He must have gotten wind of the fact that you were on Destiny Key yesterday and he sent one of his guys out to deal with you."

"You think Chief Tyler is the murderer?" I asked.

"I do. And he's going down for it if it's the last thing I do."

I turned on the engine, quickly lowering the radio volume so he wouldn't hear what I sang along to when driving.

"He didn't do it," I said as I put the car in reverse. "Meet me at the Tipsy Pirate tonight and I'll explain. There's a going-away party for Olivia. It'll be the perfect opportunity to look the killer in the eye and make an arrest."

* * *

"Are you sure this is a good idea?" Scooter asked as he held the door open for me.

"Sure. Chief Dalton will be here and the Tipsy Pirate is a public place. No one is going to try anything." I turned and waved at a woman behind me. "Besides, the chief has one of his deputies keeping an eye on us. She seems nice, but she could smile more, don't you think?"

"She's here to protect you, not to make friends," Scooter said.

"Maybe I should introduce her to Ben," I said. "I'm not sure things are going to work out between him and Sawyer."

Scooter chuckled. "We're here because of a murder and all you can think about is setting Ben up on a blind date. Unbelievable."

"I'm also thinking about my empty stomach," I said. "Wanna split an order of egg rolls?"

"It looks like they've ordered food already," Scooter said. He pointed at a large table at the back of the bar that was covered with trays of assorted appetizers. Olivia, Sawyer, and Ben were seated at one side of the table munching on fried cheese balls. Across from them were Anabel and Chief Dalton, sharing a plate of calamari. Thomas walked over, set down a pitcher of rum punch and then sat next to Anabel.

After we ordered gin and tonics at the bar, Scooter and I joined the gang, pulling chairs up next to the chief.

Ben stood and tapped a knife on a glass. "Can I have everyone's attention? I want to make a toast to the birthday girl, Sawyer." He turned to her and smiled. "May you live to be a hundred, with an extra year to repent." After he clinked her glass and took a sip of his beer, Ben motioned to a waitress who was holding a large cake. As she carried it to the table, everyone sang *Happy Birthday.*

Scooter nudged me. "I thought this was a going-away party for Olivia."

"Looks like it's a surprise party for Sawyer as well," I said. "See, this is how you throw surprise parties. You have a cake and candles and you sing *Happy Birthday.* You don't take the birthday girl to a YouTube seminar."

"It wasn't even your birthday," Scooter said. "But don't worry, I already have a surprise lined up for you when it rolls around."

"Ooh, what is it?" I asked.

"Shush," Scooter said, ignoring my question. "I can't hear what Sawyer is saying."

The young woman was holding up a card. "Isn't that sweet? It says, 'May you always have fair wind and following seas' on the inside." She leaned over and kissed Olivia on the cheek. "Thank you. I love it. I know just where I'm going to put this up in my van."

"Can I see that?" I asked. After Sawyer handed me the card, I looked at the inscription inside. "Your penmanship is really impressive, Olivia. You could make a living doing calligraphy on wedding invitations."

"She's so talented, isn't she," Sawyer gushed. "Not only is she a sailor, an artist, and a YouTube star, but she can also do all sorts of handwriting, too."

Ben chuckled. "I should have had her forge my parents' signatures on my report cards."

Sawyer punched his arm playfully. "You should have just studied harder instead of throwing spitballs."

I pointed at the white sailboat on the front. "This looks familiar."

"That's Olivia's boat," Sawyer said.

"I have a confession to make," Olivia said. "I stole Sawyer's idea to make greeting cards using my artwork on the front. I'm going to try to sell them when I'm back in New York."

"It was actually Thomas' idea," Sawyer said. "We probably owe him some sort of commission."

Thomas laughed and held out his glass. "How about if we make it payable in rum punches?"

While Olivia refilled his glass, I tapped the chief's arm and passed him the card. "Take a close look at this," I said in a low undertone.

"What am I looking at?" he asked.

"Right there, on the bow of the boat. See what it says?" The burly man locked eyes with me, then slowly nodded. "But that's not all." I opened the card and pointed at Olivia's handwriting. "Someone had to have forged Victoria's suicide note, don't you think?"

He rubbed his jaw while he considered the implications of what I had just said. "Okay, let me think about how to handle this."

I took a sip of my gin and tonic. "How about if you let me handle this?"

Then I tapped the side of my glass to get everyone's attention. "Olivia, do you mind telling us why you murdered Gregor and Victoria?"

CHAPTER 16
HAIRBALLS

Olivia nearly spit out her drink. "Me? Murder Gregor and Victoria? Is this some kind of joke?"

Thomas frowned. "This isn't funny, Mollie. Show some respect for the dead. Victoria was a troubled soul who took her own life."

"No, she didn't." I pushed my plate to the side and leaned forward. "She was murdered."

"But she left a note," Thomas said.

"There was a note, but she didn't write it," I said. "Someone forged it."

"That can't be right," Thomas said, his brow furrowed. "There were details in there that only Victoria would have known."

Olivia snorted. "See, I didn't have anything to do with it."

Sawyer looked sideways at her friend, then asked, "What kind of details?"

"She mentioned a conversation that we had the night of the reception at the gallery," Thomas said softly. "I told

Victoria that it was wrong to let someone else take the blame for killing Gregor."

"Well, there you go," Olivia said. "How could I have known about their conversation?"

"Same way I did," I said. "Eavesdropped."

"You overheard us?" Thomas asked.

I felt my face get warm. "Uh, I happened to be standing near the Snow White topiary when the two of you started arguing. I didn't want to embarrass you by making my presence known. I'm not sure where Olivia was hiding. Maybe over by Puss in Boots."

Thomas stared down at the table. "That was the last time I spoke with my cousin," he said softly.

Olivia sized me up while she took a sip of her drink. "You're the one who overheard what they said, so it only stands to reason that you were the one who wrote that note."

"So, you're admitting that Victoria was murdered?" I asked.

"Sure, if you say so," she sneered.

Thomas pushed back his chair, stood, then started pacing back and forth next to the table. "It still doesn't make sense," he said. "She wrote about what happened between her and Gregor that night. The text from Gregor's wife on his phone, and how they fought about it. No one else would have known that except Victoria."

I shook my head. "How do we even know that's what happened? Both Victoria and Gregor are dead. Olivia could have made up any old fictitious conversation between the two of them."

"For the last time," Olivia said, slamming her glass on the table, "I didn't kill anyone." She turned to Sawyer. "Come on, let's get out of here."

Sawyer looked at me, then back at Olivia. "Maybe we should hear Mollie out."

Olivia grabbed her purse. "And I thought we were friends."

As she started to get up from the table, Chief Dalton said, "Sit back down, Miss Peterson."

"No way," she said. "I know my rights. I don't have to stand for this."

The chief nodded at his deputy. She walked over to Olivia, stared impassively at the young woman, then pointed at the chair. Olivia set her purse on the floor and meekly sat back down.

After pouring some more rum punch in her glass, Olivia leaned forward and locked eyes with the chief. "You don't have any proof. All you have is some crazy claim that Victoria's note was forged."

"That's not all we have." I picked up the birthday card from the table and pointed at the illustration on the front. "Tell us, what's the name of your sailboat?"

"The *Anastasia*," she said. "What does that have to do with anything?"

"I remembered you talking about circumnavigating on the *Anastasia* when we went to your YouTube seminar. At the time, I thought it was a pretty boat name—much nicer than *Marjorie Jane*. But I didn't really think about it much after that."

"What's wrong with *Marjorie Jane*?" Scooter asked.

"It's kind of dull, don't you think?" I replied.

"People rename their boats all the time," Ben said. "You should think about it. How about the *Black Pearl* or—"

Chief Dalton held up his hand. "Perhaps we should get back to the subject at hand."

I nodded. "You're right. What were we talking about? Oh, yeah, the name *Anastasia*. I heard it again when Melvin and I were at Destiny Key yesterday. We met a man who looks just like Colonel Sanders."

Ben chuckled. "That would be a great boat name. Instead of a mermaid figurehead at the bow, you could have one of a chicken."

"Anyway," I continued. "This guy, Silas de Vries was his name, he mentioned a Russian woman named Anastasia Petrov. She and her husband, Mikhail, were notorious art forgers. Gregor knew them. He used to sell their fakes to unsuspecting art collectors. Silas also said something else interesting. The Petrovs had a daughter named Oksana. After her parents were arrested, she changed her name and tried to make a new life for herself."

"What does that have to do with Olivia?" Sawyer asked.

"Olivia Peterson has a nice ring to it, doesn't it?" I asked. "So does Oksana Petrov. Did you know that 'Petrov' means 'Peter' in English? Like 'Peterson'? I've learned a lot about Russian over the past few days. For instance, did you know that *kroshka* means 'crumb'? That's the pet name that Gregor called Victoria." I nudged Scooter. "Much cuter than stegosaurus, don't you think?"

"Really? You'd rather be called something that has to do with a scrap of food rather than a dinosaur?" Scooter asked.

Chief Dalton cleared his throat. "Enough about pet names. Let's get back to the point."

"Fair enough." I looked at Olivia. "I can see how if you were going to change your name, it might be nice to keep it somewhat similar to your old one. It would be a way to keep a connection with your parents."

"This is ridiculous," Olivia said. "I didn't change my name."

"That's the kind of thing that can be easily checked," Chief Dalton said.

I toyed with the birthday card. "That's why you named your boat the *Anastasia*, isn't it? A tribute to your mother."

Olivia put her hands to her mouth and took a deep breath. "Even if I did change my name, and I'm not saying I did, what does that have to do with Gregor's murder?"

I grabbed my phone out of my purse and pulled up the Russian translation of the note I had found. "Gregor threatened to expose your past. He told you that if you didn't give him one hundred thousand dollars he would put a painting called 'The Dishonor of Mikhail and Anastasia' up for auction. It was a sort of code he used rather than come out and say directly that he'd spill the beans about your secret past unless you coughed up the money."

"Is that true?" Sawyer asked her friend.

When Olivia didn't respond, Sawyer pushed her chair closer to Ben and whispered something in his ear. He nodded, then put his arm around her shoulders protectively.

"When I was researching Russian names, I found out something else interesting," I said. "You know how we use nicknames in English? Like Tom for Thomas and Ben for Benjamin. Well, they do the same thing in Russian. Men named Mikhail are often called Misha for short."

"Misha sounds familiar," Ben said.

"It should," I said. "Remember when we were at that art presentation at the gallery?" Ben nodded. "Olivia was telling us a story about how her father insulted one of her friends about her snoring. She mentioned how when her mother admonished him she called him Misha."

Up until this point, Anabel had been sitting quietly next to her ex-husband. "That's confirmation that her father's name is Mikhail," she said before leaning forward and glaring at Olivia. "Do you realize that I was arrested for the murder of Gregor? Do you know what I went through? And it was all because of you!"

Chief Dalton pulled Anabel back into her chair. "Calm down. You're not helping matters."

She twisted away from him. "Aren't you going to arrest her?"

"Shush," he said, lightly touching her hand. Then he turned to Thomas. "Why don't you have a seat, Mr. Sinclair? You're going to wear out the floor with all that pacing."

"I still don't understand," Thomas said as he sat down. "I

saw Victoria on the dock that night."

"What you really saw was Olivia wearing a wig," I said. "There's a trunk full of old theatrical stuff, including costumes and wigs, at Warlock's Manor. It was easy for Olivia to disguise herself. That way if anyone saw her at the dock, they would have mistaken her for Victoria."

Thomas rubbed his face. "I guess that could have been the case."

"Do me a favor and think back to that night," I said. "You came downstairs to check on the generator. You went into the drawing room and looked out the bay window. That's when you saw a woman that looked like Victoria, right?" He nodded. "Did you see her face?"

"No," he admitted.

"When you were in the drawing room, did you see anyone sleeping on one of the couches?" Thomas shook his head. I looked at Sawyer. "At the art presentation, Olivia told Ben and me that your allergies were bothering you and that you were snoring."

Sawyer's face reddened. "Snoring? I don't snore."

"Mollie snores sometimes, too," Scooter said with a smile.

"I don't snore," I said. "I purr. It's like how woman don't sweat, they glow. Anyway, it doesn't matter whether you were snoring or purring, Sawyer. What matters is that Olivia said that she went to sleep in the drawing room that night because of the noise. But Thomas didn't see her when he was in there."

"That's because she was standing on the dock," Thomas said slowly.

"Correct. She arranged to meet Gregor that night to discuss his demand. Then she killed him with his own knife. She pushed him into the dinghy, then untied it from the dock, hoping it would float away somewhere into the mangroves where no one would see it. What she didn't count on was the stern anchor falling out, catching on the bottom, and preventing it from drifting away."

"There's no way I would have been that stupid," Olivia scoffed. "You forget that I'm an experienced sailor. I would have made sure that the stern anchor wasn't deployed."

"You had just killed someone. People make mistakes in the heat of the moment." I leaned forward. "It's understandable why you did what you did. Gregor wasn't a nice man. He was threatening to expose your parents for what they were—second-rate artists who couldn't cut it on their own, so they painted forgeries instead."

Olivia pounded the table with her fist. "My parents weren't second rate!" She pointed at Thomas, Sawyer, and Anabel, each in turn. "Not like all of you. None of you has half the talent that they had. They could have made a name for themselves if it wasn't for people like Gregor. He blackmailed them into painting forgeries. He ruined their lives and he ruined mine. Do you know what it's like being an eighteen-year old-girl and seeing your parents arrested? He deserved to die! And so did that insipid woman, Victoria. A chimpanzee could have painted better than she did. I did her a favor by destroying her paintings."

Thomas lunged across the table and grabbed Olivia. "You killed my cousin," he said, shaking her by the shoulders before collapsing back into his chair and sobbing.

Chief Dalton rose to his feet and walked over to the young woman. "Olivia Peterson, I'm placing you under arrest for the murder of Gregor Smirnov and Victoria Williams."

After he read Olivia her rights and escorted her out of the bar, we all sat in silence for a few minutes.

"Anyone want another drink?" Ben asked.

After the waitress brought us over another round, I asked Thomas if he wouldn't mind clearing up something. "When I was at Warlock's Manor yesterday, I found a piece of Gregor's cane in the fireplace. Were you trying to burn it?"

Thomas ran his fingers through his hair. "You have to

understand. I thought Victoria had killed Gregor. After I saw her that night...or at least, I thought I saw her, I went back to bed, but I couldn't sleep. So I got dressed and went out for a walk before dawn. It was foggy out so I took a flashlight with me. Without realizing it, I found myself on the dock. That's when I saw the bottom of Gregor's cane. I picked it up, then shone the light out on the water."

"You saw Gregor in the dinghy, didn't you?" I asked.

Thomas sighed. "I did. That's when I suspected Victoria."

I tapped Scooter's arm. "Remember when we saw Jim at the Sailor's Corner Cafe earlier this week and he slipped up and said something about Thomas discovering Gregor's body?" Scooter nodded. "Then he tried to cover it up, saying that he meant Thomas had seen the body." I turned back to Thomas. "You told Jim about it, didn't you?"

"Uh-huh. We fought about it. He thought I should go to the police, but I..." His voice trailed off.

Anabel squeezed his hand. "You were trying to protect your cousin. She was family. We get it."

Scooter held up his glass. "Let's make a toast. To Victoria. May she rest in peace."

* * *

A couple of days after Olivia's arrest at the Tipsy Pirate, Scooter, Mrs. Moto, and I were standing on the marina patio chatting with Penny when Nancy stuck her head out of the office door. "You have a package in here," she barked. "It's been sitting here for over five days. If it isn't claimed by the end of the day, it's going in the dumpster as per Section 27(d)."

I rolled my eyes and handed the calico to Scooter. "I better go get it."

When I walked into the office, Nancy was on the phone explaining to someone how electricity was metered at the docks. On the other side of the room, Melvin was tacking something up on the bulletin board. When he saw me, he handed me a flier. "Check out this contest we're running at the Marine Emporium in conjunction with one of our suppliers."

My jaw dropped as I looked at it. "The first prize is a brand new dinghy and an outboard engine."

"You and Scooter should enter," he said. "You seem to be one lucky gal. I don't know anyone else who could get away with half the stuff you do. That guy almost killed you at the nature reserve."

"I know," I said. "If it hadn't been for that young family saving the day, I might not be here."

"Exactly," Melvin said, tapping his finger on the flier. "Maybe your luck will extend to winning a dinghy and outboard."

"What's this about almost getting killed, dear?" Nancy asked as she smacked her fly swatter on the counter.

"Remember Chief Tyler's henchman?"

The older woman nodded.

"Well, he sent one of them after me to keep me from nosing into his business."

"But he didn't have anything to do with Gregor and Victoria's murders," she said.

I shook my head. "No, he was worried that I knew too much about potting soil."

"You never struck me as being someone who had a green thumb," Nancy said.

"I don't. But Michael, the guy who owns Warlock's Manor, is a master gardener. Apparently, they have an annual flower competition on Destiny Key. Michael always wins, which makes Chief Tyler's wife livid. She told him to do something about it, in no uncertain terms."

"That seems a bit extreme to have sent someone kill you over a flower competition," Melvin said.

"I know," I said. "But everyone keeps telling me what a strange place Destiny Key is."

"Aren't you worried that he's still going to come after you?" the older man asked.

"No. It turns out that some of the more powerful residents of Destiny Key are no long enamored with Chief Tyler. They feel that he's drawing too much attention to the island and interacting too much with folks from the mainland. Apparently, he's been 'taken care of.' And before you ask, I'm not sure what that means, but I've been assured that he won't be bothering me or anyone else again."

"How do you know all this?" Nancy asked.

"Thomas spoke to Michael yesterday to catch him up on everything that happened while he was in Europe." I leaned forward on the counter. "Anyway, we saw Chief Tyler stealing some sacks from Michael's garden shed and putting them in his vehicle. Turns out it was magic potting soil."

"Magic soil," Nancy scoffed. "Whoever heard of such a thing?"

"I just know what Thomas told me. It's one part mushroom compost, one part peat moss, one part pine bark, and one part magic pixie dust." I smiled as I recalled the glitter I had seen when the potting soil spilled out in our dinghy. "Purple magic pixie dust," I added.

"He's pulling your leg, dear. There's no such thing as pixie dust." She reached under the counter and pulled out a cardboard box. After I signed and initialed a four-page release form, she handed the package to me.

When I walked back outside, I saw Mrs. Moto sprawled on a table, purring loudly while Penny scratched her belly. "What did you get?" she asked.

"I don't know. I didn't order anything," I said. "It's addressed to Scooter."

I set the box on the table and started to tear it open. Scooter grabbed it away from me. "Hey, that doesn't have your name on it."

"I thought we didn't have any secrets between us," I said with a smile.

"It's a surprise. You can open it on your birthday."

"But that's not for ages. I can't wait that long." I pointed at the cat, who was using her claws and teeth to rip the tape. "I don't think Mrs. Moto can either."

Scooter grinned. "All right. Go on and open it."

"There's t-shirts in here," I said once I got the box open.

He pulled out a large navy blue shirt and held it up against his chest. "This one is for me."

"What does that say?" Penny asked as she leaned forward. "I'm not in charge. Ask the admiral," she read out loud. "That's funny. I see there's an arrow pointing to the right. I bet you have one in here for Mollie that says she's the admiral. When you stand next to her, your t-shirt points at her."

"Not exactly," Scooter said, handing me a woman's version of the t-shirt.

"It says the same thing—'I'm not in charge. Ask the admiral.' But my arrow's pointing to the left," I said.

"Ta-da," Scooter said as he pulled out a tiny t-shirt. He picked up Mrs. Moto, pulled it over her head and front paws. Then he held her up. "See, it says, 'Ask me. I'm the admiral.'"

The calico meowed loudly.

"I think she likes it," Penny said.

"Yep," I said. "But we're going to have to make sure being an admiral doesn't go to her head. First YouTube, then commanding a ship." I scratched Mrs. Moto behind the ears. "What's next for you, kitty-cat? World domination?"

She replied by hacking up a hairball on the table.

Penny burst out laughing. "The admiral has spoken."

Scooter put his arm around me and kissed my forehead. "Happy early birthday," he said. "I hope you like your present."

"I love it," I said. "I think they'll be the perfect crew shirts for all of us to wear when we go sailing to the Bahamas."

Scooter pulled back and looked me in the eye. "The Bahamas? Did I hear that right?"

"Yep. What do you say? Should we head off to the Bahamas after Christmas?" I held up my hand. "I'm not saying we're going to sail around the world, just the Bahamas. Deal?"

"Deal," he said, shaking my hand before picking up Mrs. Moto and whispering in her ear. "Did you hear that? We're going to the Bahamas!"

MOLLIE'S SAILING TIPS

I asked Mollie if she wouldn't mind sharing some thoughts on the name of her boat and what would be involved if she and Scooter decided to rename it. Here's what she had to say.

RENAMING YOUR BOAT

When Scooter presented me with a sailboat named *Marjorie Jane* for our tenth wedding anniversary, let's just say that I didn't exactly jump for joy. It wasn't the diamond necklace I had been hoping for. But over time, she's grown on me. Part of that has to do with the fact that I've learned how to sail and love it. The other part of it is because I've invested a lot of sweat, time, money, and tears into fixing her up. When you've invested so much of yourself into a project, you either end up loving it or hating it. While I wouldn't say that I love *Marjorie Jane*—at least not out loud—I would say that I'm fond of her.

But what I'm still not crazy about is her name. Marjorie and Jane are perfectly fine names. I know people with those names and they're really nice ladies. But it's not the name I would have chosen. Scooter and I have been discussing whether or not we should rename her. We're having a little bit of a debate about what to call her. I'm partial to *Millennium Falcon*, *Battlestar Galactica*, *Enterprise*, or *Firefly*. Scooter wants to go with something a little less exciting like *Freedom*, *North Star*, or *Endless Summer*. Mrs. Moto has also chimed in with her suggestions—*Cat's Meow*, *Cat Tales*, or her personal favorite, *Admiral Moto*.

We're still not sure whether we will rename our boat or not, or if we can even agree on a name, but in the meantime, I've been researching how you go about it.

Turns out that there's a ceremony you need to go through to ensure that you don't have bad luck. Sailors can be a pretty superstitious bunch. It actually sounds like a lot of fun because you basically throw a party, and who doesn't love a good party?

*　*　*

Poseidon, the Greek god of the sea, keeps a book (the Ledger of the Deep) with the names of all the boats in the world. He's one of those gods you don't want to cross. Go ahead and rename your boat without consulting him and bad things will happen. Your boat could be swallowed up the sea, you could have a fire down below, you could collide with another boat, or someone could be injured.

You need to consider the best day of the week for the renaming ceremony. Fridays are generally considered to be bad luck by sailors and Thursdays are often avoided because that's Thor's day and you don't want to mess with the Norse god of storms and thunder.

Step 1 – Call upon Poseidon to give your boat his blessing.

Step 2 – Offer thanks to Poseidon for protecting your boat in the past.

Step 3 – Remove all vestiges of your boat's old name.

Step 4 – Pour wine, champagne, or sparkling cider in the water from east to west.

Step 5 – Rededicate your boat with her new name to Poseidon by laying a branch of green leaves at the bow and breaking a bottle of wine, champagne, or sparkling cider across the bow. Say, "I name this ship _______, and may she bring fair wind and good fortune to all who sail on her."

Step 6 – Share the rest of the wine, champagne, or sparkling cider with your guests while standing at the bow of your boat.

Step 7 – Take everyone out for a maiden sail knowing that the god of the sea is looking out for you. Be sure to stop by Penelope's Sugar Shack first and pick up some brownies and cookies to feed your guests.

AUTHOR'S NOTE AND ACKNOWLEDGMENTS

Thank you so much for reading my book! If you enjoyed it, I'd be grateful if you would consider leaving a short review on the site where you purchased it. Reviews help other readers find my books and encourage me to keep writing.

My experiences buying my first sailboat with my husband in New Zealand (followed by our second sailboat in the States), learning how to sail, and living aboard our boats inspired me to write the *Mollie McGhie Sailing Mysteries*. You might say that there's a little bit of Mollie in me.

One of the things I like about being a writer is weaving in my own experiences into my books. You may have noticed the references to hurricanes throughout *Dead in the Dinghy*. Living on a sailboat in Florida means that we're always keeping an eye out on the weather, especially during hurricane season.

While I was writing *Dead in the Dinghy*, Hurricane Dorian was barreling through the Bahamas. We have many happy memories of our time sailing in these beautiful islands and it was absolutely awful to see the devastation that Dorian brought to this wonderful country and its people. Having Melvin refer to his past experiences losing loved ones to hurricanes was a nod to this tragic event.

I want to thank my husband, Scott Jacobson, and my good friends, Duwan Dunn and Greg Sifford, for reading earlier drafts and providing insightful and thoughtful feedback, as well as their unfailing support and encouragement. Many thanks as well to my editor, Beth Balmanno of By the Book, who was a pleasure to work with on this project.

For updates on new releases, my current projects, sales and promotions, and other fun stuff, you can sign up for my newsletter at ellenjacobsonauthor.com/newsletter.

ABOUT THE AUTHOR

Ellen Jacobson is a chocolate obsessed cat lover who writes cozy mysteries and romantic comedies. After working in Scotland and New Zealand for several years, she returned to the States, lived aboard a sailboat, traveled around in a tiny camper, and is now settled in a small town in northern Oregon with her husband and an imaginary cat named Simon.

Find out more at ellenjacobsonauthor.com

ALSO BY ELLEN JACOBSON

Mollie McGhie Cozy Sailing Mysteries

Robbery at the Roller Derby
Murder at the Marina
Bodies in the Boatyard
Poisoned by the Pier
Buried by the Beach
Dead in the Dinghy
Shooting by the Sea
Overboard on the Ocean
Murder aboard the Mistletoe

Smitten with Travel Romantic Comedies

Smitten with Ravioli
Smitten with Croissants
Smitten with Strudel
Smitten with Candy Canes

North Dakota Library Mysteries

Planning for Murder